The Gа

Zoe Chamberlain

Published by Accent Press Ltd 2014

ISBN 9781783751358

Prologue

The toadstools appeared at the bottom of the garden on the tail end of a wet and windy August. They were tiny, insignificant to start with, but in less than a week they'd grown to the size of tea-plates.

It was Rosemary who noticed them first.

We hitched up our skirts and waded through the long grass to take a better look. They were bright white, the colour of freshly fallen snow. For an entire week after their arrival, the sun shone over our home and there was not a cloud in the sky.

Then everything changed. I should have known it would.

But I didn't spot the signs, back then.

Chapter One

The town of Ivory Meadows was postcard pretty. It seemed the perfect place in which to escape and hide. I thought it would be a safe haven for me and my daughter, Rosemary.

But trouble seemed to follow me like a stranger in a hooded cloak, lurking in the shadows, waiting ready to pounce. This was something of a nuisance, seeing as all I wanted was a quiet life.

Let me explain.

The day Rosemary and I arrived in Ivory Meadows, we found it brimming with banners and Union Jack flags, bunting zig-zagged across the street from every roof top, dancing happily in the breeze. Fairy lights twinkled over the crumbling little bridge, their reflection in the river lighting up the grey summer's day. It was as if the place hadn't changed a bit in hundreds of years. Many of the black-and-white timber buildings were clearly in need of urgent repair and yet the whole place felt alive and breathing and beautiful. It felt good to be there. It felt for the first time in as long as I could remember like I, too, was alive and breathing, maybe even beautiful.

Ladies hovered in rows along the pavement with their daughters, being careful not to dirty their best dresses, while men and boys chatted nearby in their hats and suits.

A large imposing church stood right in the centre of the town, like an island in the midst of the tiny road running around it, shops lining each side of the street. The road was, for some reason, closed to traffic today. The walls of the church had been blackened by the passing of time and exhaust fumes, but it had a pretty bell tower and a huge stained-glass window, across which an enormous banner had been hung, saying 'Welcome Home!' A pretty flowerbed of roses stood just in front of the church, shielding it from the cars. The entrance was a battered old wooden door to the shady side of the church, opposite a hardware shop.

Stood on the pavement outside the shop was a large man wearing a white apron, which was splattered with blood. His enormous hands were wrapped around his rotund belly as he watched the townsfolk gather. In spite of his forbidding demeanour, he had a kind face with heavyset features that seemed to smile without his lips moving. I guessed from his apron that he must be the local butcher and stopped to ask him what the celebration was in aid of.

'Vicar and his new wife are coming home from honeymoon,' he said, in a strong country accent.

'Oh, I see,' I said, not sure that I did.

'Used to be tradition, back in Georgian times when the town was built, that when a local clergyman married while in office, the whole town would be decorated to welcome the happy couple home.

'Reverend John Baker's done a lot for our town so we decided to bring back the custom as a surprise for him.'

'That's a lovely thing to do,' I said to the butcher.

'You think?' he asked, raising his eyebrow. 'The supermarket chains tried to close me down, as they did the greengrocers, Dennis and Barbara Sullivan, Mr Morris from the hardware store, and Gillian the florist.

'The vicar managed to persuade the local people to continue to shop at home rather than being tempted away by cheaper, substandard food and free parking.'

'Has it worked?' I asked.

'Oh it's working all right but it's taken a good year,

4

mind. There was them stubborn types who wouldn't budge, thought development and progress was good for the town. Good for Ivory Meadows? That's a lot of pantomime good for the town, more pantomime good for their pockets.'

He winked at me and I smiled, grateful to him for not cursing in front of Rosie.

'But it's working; as I say, it took a good long time and we nearly had to knock it on the head but it's working.' There was a pause as I waited for him to continue. 'As I say, we've got a lot to thank him for.'

Suddenly, there was a loud shout and everyone around us started to clap and cheer. The butcher immediately broke into a run, as if he'd heard a wild bull was charging over the hill. He darted across the road, and into the church, faster than his size looked able. Within seconds, a peel of bells echoed in the street.

'They must be home,' I said to Rosie, lifting her up so she could get a better view across the scores of people lining the street down to the bridge over the river.

We watched as the vicar and his wife got out of their car in front of the church, looking somewhat bewildered. The crowd flocked around them, shaking the clergyman's hand, patting him on the back and kissing his wife. The couple waved, said thank you, then took one look at each other and bolted for the car, locking the doors and driving quickly through the crowds round the church and up the vicarage drive.

It seemed ungracious, considering all the trouble the townsfolk had gone to. He didn't seem half the character the butcher had built him up to be.

'Don't like a fuss, the vicar, that's his way,' said the butcher, who was now back at my side.

'I'm sorry,' I said, 'My name's Vivian, Vivian Myrtle.'

'Pleased to meet you,' he said, 'm'name's Bill but you

can call me whatever you like.' And with a twinkle in his eye he was gone.

We made our way up the hill to our new home, Rosie, arms outstretched as if she were a bird and me tottering behind, trying to catch up in precariously high heels. I hadn't had the chance to pack anything more sensible and, in any case, I kind of liked them. We'd left behind almost everything we'd owned, such had been our great rush to get out of London. The two of us had certainly stood out from the crowd. Rosie looked like a ray of light in her yellow T-shirt with her long, curly, red locks streaming out behind her as she ran. She barely looked like me. My features were dark, with my thick wavy hair generally a mop on top of my head within minutes of my combing it. I kept it short to try to tame it but it made little difference. Catching up, I grabbed Rosie and spun her round. With the sun setting behind her head, she looked like an angel.

I hoped I hadn't forgotten the way home. I knew it wasn't far from town but it was a very steep hill. It had been a long and tedious journey that morning from London, firstly by train, then by taxi, which seemed somewhat extravagant considering our severe lack of finances. We popped into the local estate agents to collect the keys and had tried to follow their instructions to our new home but failed miserably. I had never been blessed with a sense of direction. Luckily, we stumbled into a stern but pleasant enough elderly lady who offered to guide us there, taking us through more fields than I cared to remember, before pointing out a wooden gate, strewn with brambles, then promptly disappearing before I even had chance to thank her.

Cherrystone Cottage, our new home, stood in a clearing in the middle of a dense forest. If you didn't know about its small latticed gate, you'd have never known it was there. We'd arrived, plonked down our bag bearing

6

just a single change of clothes each on the kitchen table, and headed straight back into town to grab some chips for dinner. We wolfed them down, our fingers shiny with grease, suddenly realising it felt like an eternity since we'd last eaten.

Returning now at dusk, our little cottage was even trickier to spot. Feeling in the undergrowth, we found the gate and it creaked open. The whole forest seemed to stir. The damp, dusk air suddenly filled with the intoxicating scent of honeysuckle and jasmine that grew along the path. At the bottom of this path stood our home, the prettiest house I'd ever seen. More than two hundred years old, the cottage was the colour of buttermilk and surrounded by cherry orchards.

Even though it was mid August, we were both shivering in the shady glade so we ran up the path to the back door. We'd already learnt that morning that it was impossible to use the front door; the overgrown ivy was holding it tight as if it didn't want to be disturbed. The back door led us into the dark, dusty kitchen, straight into the heart of the home. A huge Aga and an old wood-burner dominated the room. Next to the fireplace was a pile of freshly cut wood. I hadn't spotted it when we'd arrived first thing but someone had clearly been here not long before us.

I was unsure how to light a fire but it almost seemed to light itself and within no time the whole room was filled with a cosy orange glow. We huddled together in front of it for a while, not moving: Rosie transfixed by the dancing, spitting flames; me trying to come to terms with just how much our lives had changed in the space of a week.

In no time Rosie fell asleep and, picking her up and carrying her in my arms, I slowly climbed up the twisting staircase and, stooping so as not to bang my head on the ceiling, I shuddered as I heard the scurry of mice in the attic. As soon as Rosie had laid eyes on her room that morning, she'd taken her sleeve and, wiping the dust from the window, found she could see right the way down to the river. She immediately fell in love with it and adopted it as her own, not even mentioning the lumpy bed that lost a spring every time she bounced on it.

Lying her down, I rubbed her nose. It was covered in glitter. She always seemed coated in sparkly dust. It was as if she was made of the stuff and it poured through her skin and her hair, leaving little trails on the floor behind her.

Stepping up a couple of steps into my room, I felt a kind of peacefulness unlike anywhere else I had been. A beautiful, hand-stitched patchwork quilt lay on the bed and, as I sat down, it filled the room with dust, dust full of memories from decades past. We were home.

Bright and early the next morning, I took Rosie to Ivory Meadows Primary School, which was just ten minutes across the field and down the lane from our home. I'd spotted the pretty little primary with its brightly coloured playground from our taxi window the day before. Rosie had loved the look of it, immediately trying to guess which might be her classroom next month. Today, unsurprisingly, the place was empty as it was the school holidays but we did manage to find an out-of-hours office number taped to the pillar-box red front door. I took a note of the number then we walked hand-in-hand into town to find a telephone box. The lady in the central council office was very friendly over the phone and promised she would send me all the forms to enrol Rosie ready for the September term.

The next task on our list was to find a job for me. I desperately needed an income if we were to survive here. We'd arrived with just a handful of bank notes and, although the rent on the cottage was startlingly low compared to London prices, I knew I had to earn enough to keep us there. But most of the staff in the shops and offices we visited looked at us with suspicion and told me they had no positions vacant. Listlessly, we wandered into the greengrocers to buy some vegetables for our tea.

'Cheer up, it might never happen, love,' whispered the lady behind the counter. With permed and highlighted hair, she had a no-nonsense look about her but her big brown eyes were full of kindness and I instantly warmed to her.

'Oh, I'm afraid it already has,' I said, then smiled and told her of our unproductive day.

'Just so happens we need someone, part-time mind, but perhaps that might tide you over for a while?'

I was so happy, I could have hugged her. Rosie and I danced round the shop and repeated our thanks so many times, Barbara Sullivan, as she told us her name was, ended up blushing. In the end she bade us goodbye, telling us to clear off while she introduced the idea of a new member of staff to her rather hen-pecked looking husband, Dennis.

By the end of my first week, I had found I loved working for Barbara and Dennis at the greengrocer's shop. They kindly said Rosie could quietly play with their two youngest sons in the flat above the shop while I worked, just until the school term started. Barbara's mum came to keep an eye on the boys and she said she enjoyed having a girl around the house a few days a week. Rosie loved her time with Ben and Charlie. And she was good as gold, making us all beautiful paintings which Barbara graciously put up around the shop. When it was quiet, Rosie was able to come downstairs and help pack apples, berries, and potatoes into their right boxes on the shelves. The shop was something of an Aladdin's cave, an old-fashioned place with drawers behind the counter full of spices and different blends of coffee. There was also loose tea leaves, peppercorns, caraway seeds, nutmeg and chilli powder, each with its own little scoop tucked inside so as not to confuse the flavours. Rosie and I concocted stories that they were elusive potions shipped in in carpet bags from overseas then sold surreptitiously on street corners for vast sums of money. Of course, in reality, they were everyday household food stuffs as the people of Ivory Meadows had no desire for the exotic. In fact I soon learned they were generally suspicious of anything brought in from outside the town, let alone overseas.

At home, Rosie adopted a stray cat and called him Whisper because she said he told her lots of secrets. My mother had always said a strange black cat in the house was a sign of prosperity so I told Rosie he could stay until we found his rightful owner.

Rosie and I had grown to love walking in the woods and fields near to Cherrystone Cottage. It was so peaceful and quiet and yet there was so much to see and enjoy at the same time. The forest was an enormous 8,000 acres, full of oak, beech, and birch trees, their leaves rustling in the wind, sharing the tales they clung onto from hundreds of years before like circles of haggard old women, waving their twisted fingers at each other. We often walked barefoot, the mosses and lichens creating a luxurious carpet on the forest floor. High up above, the elm trees stood so tall they looked like stairways to the sun. I was tempted to hitch up my skirt and climb as far as I dared then sit, arms outstretched, pretending I could fly, just like I had done when I was a child. It was so completely different to the noisy, dirty city life we'd been used to.

We were becoming familiar with the bird-songs, and were able to spot the difference between the voice of a starling and that of a blackbird, and notice how the markings of the blue tit differed from the great tit. I loved the way the cuckoo called repeatedly after a rain shower. One day we saw a kingfisher, bright blue and beautiful, on the water's edge, and spent several minutes transfixed by his grace and extravagance before he flew off. No wonder he was said to be the first bird Noah set free from the ark.

There were foxes and rabbits and we even spotted a badger once when we were sitting very quietly, taking a moment's reflection under a big oak tree. Sometimes it was possible to catch a glimpse of fallow deer in the dark of the forest as they carefully stepped out to bask their backs in the sunlight. My favourites, though, had to be the otters, timid but captivating little creatures down by the river.

It was down at the water's edge where I finally got to talk to the vicar. We had seen him many times before during our long, quiet walks. He was a small man with rounded features and a shiny bald head. Each time he seemed troubled, stopping every so often to look up at the sky then resuming his stroll again. The first time I saw him I followed his train of view, expecting to see a bird or a butterfly, but there was nothing. I realised he was probably talking with the Almighty and decided it would be dreadful if he thought I was spying on him so, with some deliberation, I went over to say hello. He passed vague pleasantries then made his apologies and scuttled away. We started to see each other regularly on our walks, all of us waving but not stopping.

Then one grey afternoon, around two weeks after our arrival, Barbara kindly invited Rosie to Ben's ninth birthday party and ushered me off to 'enjoy a little time to myself'. It was strange not to have my little girl by my side. But I decided to take a walk through the forest just like I normally did with Rosie. I saw the vicar down at the edge of the river. I went and sat on the riverbank, and he immediately edged behind a tree so I could not see his face. I had a feeling he wanted to talk.

'It's admirable how Bill and the Sullivans and everyone fight so hard to keep this town traditional,' he said. His voice had a nervous, rasping lilt that made him sound like he was gasping for air as he spoke.

'Only with your help,' I said.

There was a pause, and I got the impression he had clasped his head in his hands. His voice quivered further as he whispered: 'I'm in a real mess. You see I've made a deal. I've made a deal with the … the mayor.'

It was like we were in a confessional box only our roles had changed. I had never been to confession so I didn't know if I should speak. I remained silent, listening.

'The bishop told me that this town, due to its ageing population, was getting too small to warrant its own vicar. The young people don't want to stay and the older generations are, well, passing on. I was told the neighbouring vicar of Windhook, the next town down from here, would preside over both towns.

'I was devastated. They said they would no longer pay for me or my house, and had great plans for me in another blossoming town some hundred miles south.

'But Ivory Meadows has a hold over people. It got to me and I couldn't face leaving. The mayor, Mr Johnson, was aware of my dilemma and said he wanted me to stay for the sake of the town. He offered to pay my rent for me at the vicarage, saying it was his way of serving the Lord. I was embarrassed but I could see no alternative. He's a wealthy man, so I accepted. The bishop seemed happy enough that I was being funded by charitable donation, and pretty much left us to it.

'A couple of months later, Mr Johnson visited me at home. He said he'd done a lot for me and now it was time for me to do something for him in return. I was so indebted to him for all his kindness, I agreed unquestioningly.

'He told me he was being paid by developers to bring Ivory Meadows to a close so the town could be bulldozed and turned into an area of executive riverside apartments and chain stores. The plans included hacking down half of the forest to make way for plush residential estates.

'And,' his voice trembled and he muttered in a barely-audible whisper, 'he said that I was to help him.'

I sat back on the bank, dumbfounded, but before I could say anything, he continued, 'I refused, of course, saying it went against everything I believed in, everything the town stood for, everything I thought he stood for.

'He said, "Who do you think has paid for the new roof on the church? And who do you think is paying for your house?"

'I was horrified. I was so ashamed I felt sick to my stomach. The mayor threatened to tell everyone in the town I had been paid off by the developers unless I worked with him to try to convince the local people that development was the way forward and that we should start flattening some of the old buildings to make way for the new.

'He threatened to tell my wife. I love my wife. I couldn't break her heart by letting her know I wasn't the man she thought I was.'

I felt a lump in my throat. I could relate to that.

'What could I do?' he added. 'I began to spread the word that it was God's will for Ivory Meadows to change. But Bill, the Sullivans, and Gillian the florist, especially Gillian, they only hear what they want to hear and they twist my words to make it sound like I'm saying the opposite. The local people here lead a simple existence. They don't understand.'

'But what about the welcome home party?' I asked.

'Oh, that.' He sighed. 'It was an amazing thing for them to do for me and I was really grateful. At the same time I was ashamed because I didn't deserve it. My wife couldn't understand my reaction but I saw the mayor in the crowd when I got out of my car and I knew I had to get out of there.'

A raven cawed loudly in a nearby tree. It made the

vicar jump and he turned and looked at me for the first time. He had tears in his eyes. He mumbled something about saying too much and got up with a start.

'Oh, I forgot to say,' he added, turning back, 'there was a man in the town this morning asking for a woman who sounded just like you.'

I know he saw me flinch, I couldn't help it.

'I told him I was very sorry but I didn't know of any woman who matched his description. I hope you'll repay me the same favour?'

'Thank you,' I said. 'And don't worry, I won't breathe a word of our conversation to anyone.'

And with that he scuttled away across the field into the distance.

I couldn't believe what I'd just been told. Everyone in the town would be devastated if they knew the truth.

Then it hit me like a blow to the head … 'a man was asking for you.' I felt the blood drain from my body then I panicked. Rosie. What if he'd already got to her?

I ran towards Barbara's flat, gasping for breath, my mind a blur.

Chapter Two

Rosie was there in Barbara's kitchen, playing, just where she should be. I stood in the hallway, peering in at the brightly lit room where she was messily making pizza with the boys, and I was filled with an overriding sense of emptiness. My life would have no meaning, my existence would be unnecessary, if she weren't here. Stepping into the kitchen, I picked her up and held her close. She hugged and kissed me back for a moment, then struggled to be released. I couldn't show her my fear. So I put her down, straightened my hair, and composed myself.

'They've arrived,' she said, mischievously.

I froze to the spot. 'Who has?' I asked, trying to keep the panic out of my voice.

'The fairies. The toadstools appeared this morning in the garden. That's their home,' she said, hands on hips, ridiculing me for not already knowing.

'Oh,' I said, relieved, 'let's see when we get home.'

By the time we'd helped Barbara clean up, and said our goodbyes and thank-yous, it was getting late. We made our way back up the hill, Rosie recounting how Ben's dough became too sticky and how Barbara's eldest son, Scott, had turned up late, after being out with his friends, then showed off by making an excellent pizza, topped with 'olives and everything'.

'He's sixteen, you know,' she said, as if she was the most grown-up girl in the world to be friends with someone so old.

15

She was not about to let me forget the toadstools so we waded through the damp overgrown grass down to the weeping willow tree at the bottom of the garden. As we approached, the moon seemed to illuminate the toadstools, making them shine like bright white balls of cotton wool. They were nestled together in a cluster, as if they were hatching a plan, and hiding it beneath their umbrella-shaped heads. Each had a ring of flesh around its stem that looked like a medieval cuff. It gave them an air of grandeur. I could see why Rosemary thought they were fairy homes; they did have a magical element to them.

I gathered her in my arms and cuddled her tight, watching the first stars of the night appear in our enchanted garden: 'Star light, star bright. First star I see tonight. I wish I may, I wish I might, have the wish I wish tonight.'

The following week the sun shone continuously over Cherrystone Cottage, compensating for the unusually gloomy summer we had endured.

It was Rosie's seventh birthday and I put all thoughts of what I'd been told by the vicar out of my head to mark the celebration with her.

'Lucky seven,' I told her, planting a kiss between her eyes. She danced round the garden in a strange hopping, jumping, excitable manner until I grabbed her hands and we spun round and round until we both fell on the grass in a big bundle of laughter and love. We had jelly and ice-cream all down our dresses and cake crumbs in our hair but it didn't matter. We were happy. Looking back, it was like the calm before the storm.

Getting ready for winter, I baked and baked, filling the house with smells of ginger cake, apple pie, beef stew, chicken casserole, fruit cakes, damson wine, elderflower cordial, blackberry wine, and vegetable soup. There were jars and jars of black cherry jam, bottles of cherry wine, and tins and tins of cherry cake and cherry tarts from our garden's harvest. The scent of the cooking seemed to waft down the path and into the town, such was the intensity of my baking. I don't know why I did it. But instinct told me to stock up on sunshine flavours for the larder and the freezer as it was going to be a hard winter.

My mother had taught me to cook, and to sew, skills I'd forgotten I had in my busy city life. Now it was like I was driven to cook, to be in my kitchen, by some external force, to the extent that my hands were stained black with cherry juice and I could barely keep my eyes open for lack of sleep. But oh, how I loved it! It was like an addiction. I'd forgotten how good it felt to be creative, to create not destroy.

Rosie clearly followed in her grandmother's footsteps, too. She was a natural in the kitchen. Each time we put something new on the stove, the house seemed to fill with laughter, every time a dish went into the Aga, the cottage became so warm and cosy it glowed. After nearly a week, the vegetables seemed to chop themselves and the cakes rose perfectly without us having to keep checking them. The oven hummed as if it were singing its favourite song.

Rosie was convinced it was fairies at work in the house. I sometimes joked along with her. Things certainly did seem to happen more easily here than anywhere else we'd been. Maybe Rosie was right. Maybe there was some kind of spirit in the house. It was over two hundred years old, who were we to expect nothing to have happened here before we arrived? Who were we to tamper with what was already there?

The time soon came for Rosie to start school. Barbara had kindly passed on some hand-me-downs from one of the mums at school who'd been having a clear-out over the summer. She looked pretty as a picture in her grey skirt, white shirt and socks, and navy cardigan, even though the sleeves had to be rolled back. She settled in well at school, saying Ben and Charlie had introduced her to lots of their friends in the playground. I was glad, however, that she did seem to keep herself to herself. I was so proud of how well she'd coped with our upheaval that I took her to the charity shop in the town for a treat. We spent ages trying on clothes and laughing at ourselves in the mirror. Eventually, finding three winter outfits each and coats that fitted us well, together with some warm scarves, hats, gloves, and boots, I parted with my hard-earned cash and we made our way back home with bags full of clothes. At least this went some way towards filling our empty wardrobes.

Once Rosie was in the swing of country school life, I knew I could no longer put what the vicar had told me to the back of mind. I'd spent many sleepless nights deliberating over his words and finally decided it was time to take action, despite my promise to him.

During my next shift at work, I asked Barbara if she thought the local people might like to come to a coffee morning up at Cherrystone Cottage.

'They'd jump at the chance,' she said, as she unpacked a box of ripe blackberries. 'Folk have been wondering about you, and most of them had never even heard of Cherrystone Cottage before you arrived. They wouldn't say as much to your face but curiosity would get the better of them and they'd all turn up.'

'The only thing is,' I said, lowering my voice, 'the vicar and the mayor mustn't know about it.'

She gave me one of her knowing looks.

'Better make it early this Sunday, then. I happen to know Mr Johnson's away for the weekend and Mr Baker – well he always spends all morning in church composing himself for the day's service. People will all want to go to church, though, so don't be upset if they all up and leave

18

before eleven.'

'That's perfect,' I said. 'Invite everyone you know to come up at ten.'

As it approached 10 o'clock the following Sunday morning, I started glancing nervously out of the window. I knew I was betraying my promise to the vicar. But hadn't he already been dishonest himself? I was grateful to him for not revealing my address but the way he said it sounded like a threat of blackmail. I was not about to be caught up in the very trap that had got him. Besides, I felt strong enough to face whatever came my way. How the local community reacted would be another matter altogether.

The floors were scrubbed, the tablecloth starched and spread, and the table was laden with ginger slices, fruit cake, banana loaf, and black cherry tarts. It did look pretty and I felt myself blush with pride. I'd allowed Rosie to take her pick then carry them up on a tray to her bedroom, asking her to quietly read her book there for an hour. Amazingly, she'd agreed.

Now it was just a matter of whether anyone would turn up. Barbara would, although if one of her sons was playing up even she might cry off. I was just wishing I'd had a telephone installed when I saw people starting to amble in through the clearing and up the side path that led to the kitchen door.

Mr Morris from the hardware store arrived first, perfectly polished as ever in a brown, pin-stripe suit, bow tie, and oil-slicked moustache.

I opened the door, perhaps a little too extravagantly, and welcomed him in. There was coffee on the stove so the room smelt as inviting as it looked as they walked in out of the blustery September weather.

Gillian, the florist, had brought her daughter Patricia who looked as sour-faced as her mother. It didn't add to

19

my confidence to see they both looked like they'd have much preferred to be elsewhere. However, I'd learnt from Barbara that Gillian had to be at the epicentre of any gossip, even though she always made out it was beneath her to be in the slightest bit interested. They plonked themselves straight down on the only two comfy armchairs and blankly refused any offer of cakes or biscuits, somehow finding preening their nails far more interesting.

The librarian, Mrs Sprockett, and her helper Janice rushed up the path, making her apologies for being late, even though she was one of the first to arrive. Mrs Sprockett was red-faced and buxom, pulling her ever-so-slightly too small cardigan tightly across her chest as she happily made a bee-line for the largest black cherry tart on the table, hurriedly telling Janice that one little cake wouldn't upset her diet.

An elderly couple slowly made their way towards the door, leaning heavily on walking sticks. I'd seen them come into the grocers but knew little else about them.

Soon there were more people than I could count. Then I saw Bill the butcher bringing up the rear. I was glad he was here. I felt I could rely on a reaction and a desire to fight back from him.

Most of them were dressed in their Sunday best, even Bill had shed his tatty T-shirt and jeans for a crisp-ish shirt and tie.

Five minutes later the kitchen was so full, people had to lean against the door. Bill lifted himself up and plonked himself on the work surface. I smiled. It helped me relax to see people felt at home here. Other men followed suit and soon there was just me left standing in the middle of them all. I knew time was pressing on. It was now or never. I glanced over to Barbara and could have sworn I saw her nod.

I cleared my throat but everyone was talking animatedly and didn't hear. Taking a little spoon, I gently tapped it on the edge of my teacup.

'Hullo, everybody. Thank you all for coming here so early on a Sunday morning. My name, for those who don't know me, is Vivian Myrtle. I invited you all here firstly to introduce myself and to get to know you better. But … there was another reason, too.'

I took a deep breath and slowly started to tell them what the vicar had told me, trying to keep any trace of scandal out of my voice. The story was bad enough without needing to exaggerate. When I came to the end, I looked around. Blank faces. Dumb-founded, I thought. Then Bill started to laugh.

'Is that it, Viv? We've known about that for months. Barbara overheard a conversation between Mr Baker and old Johnson outside her shop not long before you arrived. It didn't take long for us to put two and two together.'

'But what about the welcome-home party?' I blurted out, flustered.

There was mass sniggering.

'Oh that,' said Bill, 'That was our little way of embarrassing the vicar and, more importantly, rubbing Johnson's nose in it. Bit of one-upmanship you could say.'

For a moment I couldn't think of a word to say. I'd dragged them all up here for nothing. No, more than that, to make myself, the newcomer, look like a fool. I couldn't believe I'd been so naïve to think they wouldn't already know this vital information.

I backed against the stove, my optimism shattered. I was already small in stature, just like my little girl. Now I felt even smaller, faced with all these strangers in my kitchen. The warmth of the Aga penetrated my skin through my pink cotton dress and I thought I heard a little hiss from inside. It made me think of Rosie and her little fairies.

Resolutely, I stood tall in the room again. 'Well, then,' I said, 'something needs to be done about it.'

Everyone stopped in their tracks.

'You suggest we take on the two most powerful people in town?' asked Gillian. 'It would be like battling against the good Lord and the establishment in one blow. We wouldn't stand a chance.'

'And I for one want to make it to heaven,' said the little old lady, whose name I still didn't know. She was sat at the table cowering over a battered old walking stick, her grey hair covered by a scarf. She was dressed from head to foot in black. I'd have thought she was a widow had her poor, downtrodden husband not been perched at her side.

'Hear Vivian out,' said Barbara, willing me on. It was only then that I realised she'd worked out my plan from the start.

I cleared my throat. 'The mayor's development plans will not only turf out all of us but they'll jeopardise the beautiful natural world that envelops and protects Ivory Meadows,' I said, my voice quivering ever so slightly. Barbara nodded, urging me to continue.

'This town has a lot to offer. We just need to let people outside it know that it exists. We need to re-invent it as a tourist attraction while maintaining its traditional charm as its selling point.'

'You're no better than the mayor,' snarled Gillian, flicking her long blonde hair over her shoulder, 'you just want to make money out of us, too.'

Bill butted in. 'Listen, Vivian has a point. We can't survive as we are. We all know the community isn't getting any younger, and young lasses like Janice here rarely want to stay once they've passed their teens.'

Janice blushed at the mention of her name.

He continued, 'If we do what Vivian says, we'll be able to develop Ivory Meadows but on our terms rather than them pantomime flattening it and making it faceless.'

'That's exactly it,' I said, spurred on by his lead. 'And the way to do it is to think of new ways of bringing life to the town. We could offer nature trails and craft workshops, perhaps even a festive market in the run-up to Christmas. We could make Ivory Meadows *the* place to visit to get into the good old-fashioned spirit of the season!'

'Yes, maybe a Santa special riverboat cruise?' offered Dennis. Barbara patted his arm, a broad smile across her face.

'Ghost hunts?' whispered Janice, blushing further.

'Christmas karaoke?' said Ian, the landlord of The Mason Arms, at which everyone laughed.

'How about gourmet festive food evenings, and maybe even cookery classes?' suggested Mick, the restaurateur.

'A Christmas carnival at the start of advent?' said Gillian.

I beamed at her enthusiasm. She scowled as if she'd never meant to open her mouth.

Before she changed her mind, I continued, 'And we'd let people outside the town know by producing leaflets and posters about everything we have to offer.

'Then, in the New Year, we'd carry on doing all the activities in different themes to match the seasons.'

'Then the mayor would never get permission to bulldoze Ivory Meadows!' shouted Barbara, triumphantly.

'So you're in?' I asked, looking around me.

Everyone was nodding, excitedly.

'It's a bit of a leap of faith,' said the elderly lady, 'To turn our backs on the vicar in favour of the mad woman on the hill.'

'Mrs Donaldson always speaks her mind,' said Barbara, gently, 'take no notice, Vivian.'

'I hadn't finished,' said Mrs Donaldson, taking her stick and pointing it at me. 'I like this girl's style. She reminds me of myself when I was a young girl. Just try stopping me joining your blessed campaign.'

'Me, too,' quipped Gillian.

'Really?' I said, surprised after she'd been so critical

earlier.

'There's one thing you can be sure of with Gillian,' said Barbara, 'and that's that she's always earnest – just not always to one man at a time!'

The whole kitchen erupted in laughter, even Gillian breaking into a smirk.

'There is one problem,' said Bill, stepping down from the work surface to take to the floor. 'I don't want to pantomime on anyone's bonfire but the minute Johnson gets wind of this, he'll do everything in his power to stop it.'

'He's right, Vivian.' Barbara frowned. 'Walls have ears in this town. Ever since he arrived, he made sure he was always one step ahead of everyone else.'

'You mean he's not originally from Ivory Meadows?' I asked, surprised. I had assumed to become mayor of a town like Ivory Meadows you'd have to have lived here all your life.

'Oh no,' several people grunted in unison.

'He's just as much of a newcomer as you,' quipped Mrs Donaldson.

Barbara continued, 'It was strange. He just seemed to appear from nowhere. He was a wonderful showman, like some kind of circus ringmaster; people just liked spending time with him.

'He did some great things for this community. Sorted out a lot of our niggles, he did. It was only a few months ago that we realised the reason for his good deeds was not so much for our joint benefit as his own. Within a few days we discovered the man with whom we'd been happy to discuss our hopes and fears for the town knew far too much. I wouldn't be surprised if he knows about our meeting by sunset tonight.'

'Then,' I said, 'we must become an underground movement.'

A detailed plan fell from my lips although I had no

24

idea where it came from. Everyone listened hard. They thought it would work, and they wanted to give it a try. More than that, they promised to give it their all.

Chapter Three

When Rosie and I returned home from feeding the ducks on the river later that day, an elderly woman was waiting at the end of the path.

'I've been watching you,' she said.

'Really?' I asked, a little unnerved by her forthright manner. The last thing I needed was a spy. Looking more closely I recognised her as the kind but stern woman who had led us to Cherrystone Cottage on our very first day here. Then she had been covered up in a wax jacket, wellingtons, and a rain hat. Today, hatless, her platinum blonde hair was neatly pinned in place and heavy make-up was etched into the deep lines and furrows of her face.

'Mind if I come in?' she said, more of an announcement than a question as she promptly pushed past me and sat herself down on the chair in the kitchen.

'I can see you haven't changed the house much. I like that. Change is a bad thing. Can only bring problems. Unless, of course, the change is a new person, you know.' With this she winked at me.

'So how's your campaign going?' she asked.

I looked at her, shocked and doubly unnerved; she had not only plonked herself in my kitchen but also seemed to know far too much about me.

'News travels on the wind, my dear,' she said, as if she'd read my thoughts. 'It echoes around Metford Manor until the noise gets so loud I have to get out and do something about it.'

Metford Manor. The name rang a bell. I had seen a

picture of it, looking like a gothic castle with four turrets and a long drive leading up to it. Age seemed to have turned it black. Barbara told me it was haunted. I hadn't realised anyone actually lived there.

'Yes, Metford Manor is my home.' She sighed. 'Born and raised there so there's not much point in leaving.

'Miss Mary Metford,' she said, proudly extending her hand. 'It was my grandfather's grandfather's home – and a fine place to grow up in,' she added. A whimsical look came over her face. 'I've kept things the same in my father's memory, God rest his soul.'

I wondered how long it had been since she lost her father. She looked close to a hundred herself.

'Eighty-six, that's my age. Don't feel a day past seventy-six, though, to be honest.'

A heavy circle of pillar-box red lipstick overlapped her withered lips, giving her a capricious look of a sad clown. 'Don't need you to feel sorry for me,' she snapped. 'I'm quite capable of looking after myself on my own up there, thank you very much.'

'I can fully believe that, Miss Metford. Would you like a cup of tea and a piece of cherry cake?'

'Thought you'd never ask. I'll have four sugars in mine and make it a large slice. Mind if I smoke?'

She'd already lit up before I could answer.

'So how old is Metford Manor?' I asked as I put the kettle on the stove.

'It's pre-Georgian, so it's older and wiser than any other building in this town. It's watched this town grow up, and I should think it'll watch it fall down, too. In fact it's the reason this town got its name, not that anyone would be bothered about that now.'

'I'd like to know,' I said, gently. There was something about her abrupt, forthright manner that I found enormously comforting.

'Metford Manor was originally a riding school which

28

hosted regular shooting parties at the weekends. Did so right up until my pa popped his clogs. Most of the local people's livelihood came from Metford Manor's livery, hence the area was called Livery Meadows.

'It was beautiful when I was a child, surrounded by lush meadows, full of the prettiest flowers you ever saw – primroses, buttercups, and masses of bluebells in the spring. It looked like the whole place was covered in purple carpet. When I was a girl I used to run and play in those bluebells, hiding so my brothers couldn't find me. Anyway, where was I?'

'The town's name?'

'Oh yes,' she said, lighting another cigarette with a large silver lighter. 'As the town grew a sign was put up – this was before I was born, of course – a sign was put up, saying "Welcome to Livery Meadows" so the hunting folk from further afield could find it for their parties.

'Over time the letter "L" fell off "Livery" and nobody got around to replacing it. People began to refer to it as "Ivery Meadows" and gradually over time it stuck. But "Ivery" didn't sound right, so outsiders naturally assumed it was "Ivory".

'It's written that way on the ordinance survey maps now so I imagine that's how it will stay – even if everything else about it changes. It seems somehow appropriate now that our town is just as precious and hunted as those beautiful ivory tusks of elephants.'

She chuckled into her tea and lit another cigarette, stubbing out her last one even though it was only half smoked. Her hard features had faded, and she looked slightly melancholy through the haze of smoke.

I told Miss Metford I must check on Rosie. She'd scampered up to play in her room the moment we got home. It all seemed unusually quiet as I made my way up the creaky staircase. I opened the door to her room and there she was sound asleep on her bed, flat on her back and still fully dressed. Down at the river that afternoon she'd insisted on running from one spot to another, making sure no single duck, goose, or swan was left out at feeding time, giggling to herself as she threw them crumbs of bread and clearly assuming I had no idea about the sneaky morsels passing between her own lips. It must have quite worn her out. It wore me out just watching her. Now, gently sighing and smiling in her sleep, she looked so pretty, so peaceful. I pulled the bedcovers over her, gently kissed her forehead, and tiptoed back down the stairs.

'I've bought some old damson gin for you to try,' said Miss Metford, abruptly, as I walked back into the kitchen.

With that she hauled a dusty bottle out of her bag.

'Father made it. It had been a family tradition for years – suppose they had no other use for all the damsons in the garden so they decided to get squiffy on them instead.

'Thought all this had been drunk but I was clearing some space the other day and found ten bottles. Corked forty odd years ago, they were. I guess they'll be like rocket fuel now but I could think of no one better to try them with so I bought 'em down 'ere.'

I took it as a compliment and bought out two glasses. I guessed this wasn't the type of gin to mix with tonic.

'All right,' sighed Miss Metford, 'Let's pop the old bird open and see how she sings!'

She filled both glasses. 'Down the hatch, m'dear. 'Fraid that was always the only way with father's brew – first bottled or forty years on.'

I glanced over at her, she grimaced, and we both crooked the back of our necks and swigged the heavy liquor.

It was as if it hummed in my blood, a humming so loud it shrieked and rattled in my ears. And yet the sweet damsons made it taste so good. It was clear Miss Metford could see how I felt because she grinned, broadly and wickedly.

'The only other way with father's brew was to have another straight after. Kind of numbs the senses as it were.'

We both took another slug and I felt my head hit the kitchen table. 'I don't think I can drink anymore,' I said.

'Don't be silly girl, the night's young, you'll want more once the initial shock has subsided.'

She began to talk of how her father had spent many years cultivating the damson trees until they grew fabulously large fruit. Only at that point did he realise he didn't actually like damson pie or jam.

'All those years of hard work, of love and dedication to those spindly branches of his turned into a taste he quite despised. Instead, he decided to put the humble, vile-tasting damson to better use, turning its fruit into alcohol.

'My father liked a tipple but he begrudged paying large sums for bottles of whisky. Suddenly here was an opportunity to brew his own. He simply couldn't resist.'

Apparently his new passion became all consuming. Every day he would check the temperatures, corks, fruit, and sugar levels.

'It got to the stage we hardly ever saw him.' Miss Metford said. 'That's why it wasn't strange when he went missing for a few days. Everyone just assumed he was down in the cellar with his damsons in distress. Of course, he was. But unfortunately he was dead.'

I nearly choked on what I'd just drunk. Dead man's damson gin? Seeing that melancholy look in Mary Metford's eyes again, I grabbed the bottle and poured us both another.

'Thank you, m'dear. He certainly did a good job with this one. He'd have been proud of this.'

At this point Whisper came sauntering into the room, purring and weaving his tail around my legs. I was quite glad of the distraction.

'Ah yes, Whisper,' sighed Miss Metford.

'Is that actually his name? Rosie told me that was what he was called but I assumed she'd just made it up. Told me something about the cat knowing lots of secrets.'

'Whisper is my cat.'

I felt a shiver run down my spine. 'Oh, I'm so sorry. I haven't been feeding him, he came here of his own accord.'

'Yes, I know. I sent him here. The first day I met you I thought it looked like you could do with a friend.'

She smiled. Despite her external appearance, which frankly showed itself as being a bit of a battle-axe, she now had the look and warmth of a sweet, tender old lady. In many ways she reminded me of my own mother.

'Tell me about your mother,' she said.

It was like she'd read my thoughts.

'My mother? Well she was just my mum, quite fabulous to me really, but just my mum.'

'Every girl's mother is fabulous in her daughter's eyes. The trouble is most daughters have absolutely no idea just how dangerous a creature a mother can be.'

'Dangerous? I don't understand.'

'No, you wouldn't. Few daughters have the faintest clue how much power her mother has over her.'

'No, my mum always had the right idea. Right from the start she said my husband wasn't right for me.'

The gin whirred in my head. I hadn't a clue why I was telling a stranger about my love life but I couldn't quieten my words. They seemed to spill out of my mouth without my knowing. 'Mum said he was a low achiever, that he would stray, and that he wouldn't have my best interests at heart.'

'And that was right?'

'Well, he owned his own successful marketing company and he never had any affairs as far as I know, but he did abuse me in the end.'

'How did he abuse you?' She poured us both another.

We drank.

'It was just after Rosemary – Rosie – was born. He couldn't accept that she was a helpless little child who needed every second of my attention. I think he felt, in some way, cheated by the fact I didn't have so much time to devote solely to him. I think he felt that I neglected him, he told me I was an overzealous, paranoid mother. He wanted me to go for nice meals out, and just forget about Rosie.

'How could I do that? She's my own flesh and blood. He had no idea of my feelings for her. And it seemed he had little or no feelings of his own.'

The bottle glugged as Miss Metford poured us both another. I noticed it was half-empty but it didn't matter. It was good to talk. The blood-coloured gin seemed to dance, to sing in my ears, making me say things I never thought would leave the murky depths of my mind. It was like a mysterious potion that had a strange, tongue-loosening spell cast upon it.

'You see there were complications with Rosie. My pregnancy was fine but for some reason she decided to come into the world too early. I haemorrhaged during labour and Rosemary was whisked away from me into intensive care.

'For three days, I was unable to leave my bed to see her and, poor mite, she was not fit to be brought to me. When I finally made it to her side, I saw she was the most beautiful, most precious little girl I'd ever seen. Her perfectly formed nose, fingers, and toes didn't explain why she couldn't breathe for herself. I vowed that moment, there and then, never to leave her side again.'

'Let's have another drink,' said Miss Metford, slurring her words and spilling half of it on the table as she tried to look earnestly into my eyes. I don't think she could focus.

By this time my head was already spinning but the gin seemed to call my name. Vivian, Vivian, Vivian …

'Do you know my father made this?' she said, hiccupping.

'I know, you told me,' I slurred, smiling at her mistake.

'Did I?'

'Yes.'

We both collapsed into fits of giggles.

'You know, Mary, can I call you Mary?'

'It is my name.'

'Well, Mary if I didn't know you better, which I don't really but I will. Anyway, if I didn't know you better, despite the fact I hardly do at all. Where was I? Oh yes, I would say you've cast a spell on me.'

'What makes you think that?'

'This,' I said, raising my glass and swishing its contents over the side, 'this is a magic potion.'

And with one last gulp, my glass was empty.

'A witch can't cast a spell on another witch.'

'What do you mean?'

'You, Vivian, you are a witch just like me.'

'Arrgh, get off, I'm drunk just like you.'

'Come with me,' she said, signalling to the door.

Outside the air felt crisp and cool. It hit me like a tidal wave, nearly knocking me clean off my feet.

'Look up there,' said Mary, steadying my balance.

I drew my cardigan closer to me and gazed up at the sky.

'This is no ordinary garden, my dear,' chuckled Mary, 'this is the garden of stars. An extraordinary show of patterns, light and explosions take place above your head every single evening. And you don't even have to buy a ticket to see it.'

I sat down on the step, eyes wide, open-mouthed, watching.

Polaris danced like a woman who thinks no one is watching, Aries the ram sat steely-eyed stalking a shoal of

Piscerian fish, Capella the goat was caught by Auriga, the charioteer as he raged against the wicked Cerberus, the terrifying three-headed monster. The Gemini twins smiled down, hand in hand, gently flickering that all was well in the night sky. Corvus squawked a shrill crow's cry before diving onto the scorpion Scorpio. Oblivious to all this, the lustful Aquarius hardly noticed as she poured gallon after gallon of water into the black seas of night, her mind elsewhere with her lover.

Planets, shining steadily and bright, unlike their elusive twinkling friends the stars, wandered from one constellation to another, just as we humans move from one life to another. Had my new start been a success? Was it time to start thinking about moving on again, for Rosemary's sake as well as my own?

Being a mother doesn't mean you always make the right decisions, even though it may appear to your children that there was never any choice. Perhaps Miss Metford was right about my own mother, whose peculiar beliefs so readily filtered into my everyday thoughts, my everyday life. I knew, when I was growing up, that our neighbours thought Mum was crazy, maybe even dangerous, but she was always wonderful in my eyes. We never had much money so she did what she needed to survive. If that meant boiling up bits of hedgerow for dinner then so be it. I traced my finger around my mother's locket, the only thing I had of hers. I wore it sometimes when I felt I needed her courage. Here, Rosie and I did have a choice. It was just that sometimes there seemed there were too many stars and not enough sky.

I gently padded my way around the garden, cat-like, not wanting to disturb her from her nightly engagements. For a garden does not rest like we do at night. It's when she comes alive. Enjoying the peace of the birds' gentle slumber, the garden breathes huge sighs of relief, great waves of liberation, opening up each blade of grass to dance freely in the moonlight, unafraid of getting trampled. The trees sing softly in the breeze, a seldom-heard song of distant memories as they reminisce on how things used to be. The leaves on the path rustle excitedly, waiting to be swept up by the bountiful wind as she guides them on her wing to pastures new. And the moon herself, so round and sanguine, showers the whole garden in silvery, Utopian light.

Suddenly everything was still, waiting and watching. Then it came. Nature's own therapy: healing, cleansing, life-restoring, renewing, invigorating rain. At first it teased with individual droplets chasing each other down the path and into the pond. Then the droplets multiplied into drizzle, the sound echoing around the garden in sheer release, proving there need be no stillness in perfect tranquillity.

There was magic in this garden, just as there is in every garden. The fact that the flowers knew exactly when to bloom, that the birds knew precisely when to mate, that the bees knew how to spread exquisite colour throughout the garden by lavishing their pollen loads in just the right places.

The greatest spell of all was bestowed by the magnificent magnolia tree which stood in the centre, queen of the garden, clinging onto her precious buds until it was absolutely safe for them to open, just as a mother holds onto her children. Mother Magnolia knows her petals cannot shine if she hangs onto them for too long. Then all her watching, waiting, nurturing will have been worthless.

There would come a time when I would have to let Rosie go so that she too could grow and blossom and shine. How would I be wise like Mother Magnolia, knowing the precise moment to set my little girl free?

Everywhere I looked in the silvery mist, I saw magic. I saw it in the house, too: every time a tin of flour, eggs, butter and sugar rose into a light fluffy cake. Every time a log and match united to fill my cottage with a warm, amber glow. Every time a woman popped into the mirror to tell me how I looked. Every time I realised I'd been hiding the sun himself inside my cupboard as I cracked open the shell of an egg.

By now my hair was drenched and my skin tingled with pleasure with each gentle drop of rain. I felt cleansed, healed, just like the garden of stars.

I realised I must have been in a trance and glanced around for Mary Metford.

But she was gone.

Suddenly a cold chill took over my body. Shivering, I ran into the house. The kitchen was calm and peaceful, just as we'd left it, with one glowing, half-empty bottle of gin on the table, and two glasses beside it.

But, closing the door, I spotted a card. I lunged forward, humming to myself as I picked it up, thinking Miss Metford must have dropped something.

To my horror, it was a calling card from the mayor. How long had he been here, and how much had he seen and heard?

Chapter Four

The plan was this.

Maureen Sprockett was head librarian. Her job would be to research what community events used to be held in Ivory Meadows in bygone days so that we could work to bring them back, as a living, working, old-fashioned town.

Once she'd come up with some ideas, she would hang a sign on the church notice board. It would say: 'Come and Find Out More About What's Going On In Your Local Library'. This would be the signal to Gillian. She would go and choose some books to borrow then Maureen would slip an extra book into her collection at the counter. This book would contain a piece of paper with all her ideas listed on it.

Gillian was good at art and design. It was her job, being a florist. She would design two leaflets and two posters, telling people all about the forthcoming events in Ivory Meadows. I would come up with some words detailing why the town was under threat and why it had to be saved. I told her I would drop a piece of paper containing all those details into her grocery bag next time she came into the shop.

When Gillian's posters were complete, she would wrap them, pattern side inside, around four bunches of flowers, which Dennis would collect on his and Barbara's wedding anniversary on October 13, just under a month's time. Barbara would be delighted by her 'surprise' gift, put the flowers into water, then hide the leaflets and posters.

That day they would close the shop for the afternoon so

they could go for a long, leisurely celebration lunch. At this Dennis had complained about it being bad for business, but Barbara had rebuked him for being selfish and told him he could book them into The Mason Arms, then winked at me. Having a weekday afternoon free gave me an excuse to catch the train into the city, supposedly sightseeing, but really to take the leaflets and posters to the printers.

Mr Morris, the hardware shop owner, said he was friends with the printer and would have a quiet word beforehand, not only to alert him to the highly secret nature of what he was about to receive and ask him to be discreet but also to enquire about a discount.

Once back from the printers, I would pin a 'Lost Cat' sign to the fabulous old oak tree at the bottom of the hill just on the edge of town. The last digit of the telephone number would be to let George the bargee know how many days it would be before the leaflets were ready. At this point, he was to collect them, stowing them like contraband goods into the hidden compartments between the boat's base and its living area.

The next day George would make a big fuss in the butcher's shop, saying he had a problem with his boat's rudder and could Bill help him out? That night Bill was to drive his van down to the water's edge at Deanon's Brook, away from the lights of the town, and they would load the delivery into the back of the truck.

Bill would then hang another notice on the tree, this time saying 'Cat Found, Many Thanks' which would be a signal to Jeremy, the choirmaster, that it was time for him to pay a visit to the butcher. There Bill would give him several bags of meat, packed with leaflets and posters around the sides, carefully wrapped to keep them safe.

Jeremy would hide his stash inside the choir stalls and within the bell tower, which the vicar had made redundant since his embarrassment on returning from honeymoon.

I told them it was perfect as, if the vicar was getting suspicious, it was the last place he was likely to look.

We also needed to reach the press. Fortunately Barbara knew everyone so I said I would compile a couple of press releases and suggested she could drop them into the newspaper offices in the city after the leaflets had arrived, on the way to visiting her mum for tea so nobody would think it unusual.

We would hold meetings every Sunday afternoon, under the guise of astrology and yoga classes so that everyone could discreetly discuss their ideas or alert us to any potential problems. Maureen and Gillian were worried they would not be able to gather all the information and put together the posters in such a short space of time but I insisted to everyone we really had to move fast if we were to save the town. They nodded solemnly in agreement.

Barbara had been very encouraging when I arrived for work the day after the meeting. Luckily, she didn't seem to notice I was nursing a sore head as a result of Miss Metford's shenanigans. She said she'd never seen the people of Ivory Meadows react so positively to new ideas or to new people, for that matter. She said they were normally suspicious of new folk, and to be a single mother as I was, well that was practically unheard of. It was clear they didn't count Gillian in that equation and I didn't like to ask what had happened to her other half. But Barbara said they felt the plan was so carefully devised, it might just work and that my heart was in the right place, which was the most important thing. And, she joked, that she was delighted she got an anniversary meal out of it to boot!

The next morning, I dug out a plot near to the kitchen door and planted a herb garden. I sensed a battle ahead and knew I needed every weapon I could lay my hands upon. I created an apothecary of colours, fragrances, textures, and tastes. I planted basil to stimulate the brain, lemon balm to lift the spirits, mint to calm the nerves, coriander to beat fatigue and apathy, lavender for peace of mind, and rosemary for prosperity and friendship. I'd named my daughter after my favourite herb. The moment I'd first laid eyes on her I saw she was delicious, potent, medicinal, magical. Our surname was just coincidence but I loved the fact that, put together, her names symbolised friendship and love.

I also made a note to buy in cloves to comfort and cheer and nutmeg for confidence. If we were to take on the government and the church, a little help from Mother Nature wouldn't go amiss.

I enlisted Rosie's help in making bright, colourful posters advertising weekly yoga and astrology classes I proposed to run at Cherrystone Cottage.

'All welcome!' the poster read, 'Come and enjoy some relaxation and exercise for your body and mind. Suitable for any level. 3-4, Sunday afternoons. £1 each.'

We'd agreed the weekly 'fees' would help to cover the printing costs of the leaflets and posters.

Some of Rosie's posters became a little over-artistic with wild pictures of horses and fairies all over them. Still, at least they would be noticed.

Proud of our work, Rosie and I sat in the garden to have a well-earned cup of tea and slice of cherry pie. As the sun began to set over the hills, the entire sky turned a magnificent glowing pink. It was so beautiful, so full of hope and joy that we stayed there in the garden, watching until the first stars of the night appeared.

On my way to work the next day, after dropping Rosie off at school, I hung the posters all over the town. I even stuck one in the church vestry and on the notice board in the town hall. I asked all the shopkeepers to stick one in their windows, to which they promptly agreed.

Barbara told me the vicar had already received news of our meeting and was apparently furious we had dared to hold such an event on the Sabbath. She said the fact he had no idea what it was about made it even worse.

'Let battle commence,' she said, rolling up her sleeves.

I wasn't so jubilant, and just hoped my posters might bluff our rivals into thinking we were meeting for exercise. I had loved taking yoga classes when I worked in public relations in London. Before having Rosie, they were my twice-weekly salvation, two hour-long sessions where I had time to myself to be still and calm in the frenetic PR world of the city. I had even begun to take lessons on how to teach yoga myself but I gave them up when work became too busy, such was my whim. I just hoped I could remember a little of what I had been taught so I could share it with those who came this weekend.

At exactly 3 p.m. on Sunday, thirteen people arrived on my doorstep. It was not as many as the week before but it was enough. Barbara and Dennis brought along their youngest son, Ben, to keep Rosie company, leaving their eldest two, Scott and Charlie, engrossed in front of the TV. Rosie was delighted to see him and immediately the pair raced up to her bedroom to play. The Donaldsons came too, along with Maureen Sprockett, the librarian, and her assistant Janice, Gillian the florist, Bill, Mr Morris, from the hardware shop, and his daughter, Joan. Mr Morris apologised for the absence of his wife Yvonne, who had a cold and had decided to give today's class a miss. I gave him an elderflower blossom, with strict instructions to hang it up in a net and let it dry before giving it to Yvonne as a tea to clear her chest. The other two were the unwelcome additions of the mayor and his accomplice, the vicar.

I had to make this realistic.

'Right,' I said, trying my hardest to keep the jangle of

fear out of my voice, 'let's get started with some breathing exercises. This is called pranayama. Prana means life, energy, and vitality while ayama means regulation and control. Together they form a practice of regulating the flow of energy through the body using the breath. Pranayama is life-giving, it's what connects our inner energy with our outer energy. What we need to do is concentrate on breathing in, holding the breath, then breathing out and holding that breath. Everyone lie on the floor and breathe with me.'

They looked at me cynically but, urged by Barbara, they each found a spot.

'Right,' I continued, gaining confidence now they weren't all staring at me, 'gently close your eyes and enjoy this moment of relaxation. Breathe in, hold, breathe out, hold.'

After ten minutes, the atmosphere changed in the room. The scepticism and defiance seemed to drift away, people actually seemed to be enjoying it. I was amazed. Even Mr Johnson's face had altered; I think I even saw a real smile rather than a smirk. Encouraged, I got them up on their feet and led them through a series of simple poses. The dog pose on all fours, the kneeling child pose, the mountain pose stood on both feet, the lunging warrior pose.

I concluded the yoga session after twenty minutes and moved on to astrology. I didn't want to overexert anyone, although they seemed disappointed it had come to an end so quickly.

'OK,' I said, feeling much more positive and capable than half an hour ago, 'everyone please gather round the table in a circle.'

They did as they were told instantly.

'Here before me is an almanac, it lets us know which are auspicious days for each of us. It is governed by the moon, the stars, and our birth dates. I can read each person's individual horoscope over the course of the next few weeks but I shall only be able to do one person's at a time. Tonight I feel it's important for me to read Maureen Sprockett's. I shall perform the astrological reading in front of everyone, if that is acceptable to you, Maureen?'

Maureen nodded.

'Let us commence. Please feel free to ask any questions as we're going along. What is your date of birth, Maureen?'

'September 23, 1955,' she said. The date was actually irrelevant. I had no idea how to read full astrology, only the bare basics my mother had taught me and, in this instance, I wouldn't even be using that because all I wanted was to find out how she was getting on with the research.

'Maureen, according to Saturn's alignment with Jupiter, you are looking for something. Is that right, Maureen?'

She nodded.

'I feel more than that, I feel like you're searching. This has something to do with your history, your background, am I right, Maureen?'

She nodded, once more.

'Does this search leave you feeling bewildered, confused or unable to cope?'

Maureen shook her head. That was good.

'Ah, so the search into one's self is a positive one in this instance. How close do you feel you are to finding all that you are looking for?'

'Very close,' said Maureen, solemnly.

'That's good. Is there anything you feel you're lacking in this search?'

'Yes,' said Maureen, 'I'm struggling to correlate all the information ...'

'In your mind,' I jumped in. I didn't want her blowing our cover by being too direct. 'I see. Perhaps it would help to physically write down what you're finding, I'm feeling a strong sense someone in this room could help you with that. And that person is Mrs Donaldson. Do you think you could offer some assistance, Mrs Donaldson?'

Mrs Donaldson nodded. In fact she looked delighted. I could see she understood and would call into the library at the first opportunity she had. It was obvious that try as they might Maureen and Janice could not physically get through all the volumes of historical reference in the library between just the two of them.

'Good. That concludes the end of today's reading. We shall look at someone else's next week. Thank you all for coming; please do feel free to bring a towel or blanket to lie on next time so that you can feel as comfortable as possible.'

Everything seemed to be going to plan. While I was afraid the mayor and vicar may have enjoyed the yoga a little too much and be keen to return next week, I had little doubt they were so confused by the astrology session they would write off the whole thing as claptrap.

Meanwhile, Maureen had managed to communicate her problems to me and we had been able to resolve them without giving anything away. It seemed, with a little luck, everything was on schedule. I just needed her to remember to put up the sign on the church notice board when everything was ready but I had little fear she would forget.

I watched as they made their way back down the hill, arm in arm, until all I could hear was the odd chuckle in the distance.

I was right about the mayor. He never showed up to class again and Barbara said she'd heard him telling the vicar's wife what nonsense it was as he convinced her not to attend.

Mr Baker himself, however, needed a little more convincing. And yet, the beauty was, he found the second yoga session even more relaxing than the first and dozed off at the end, leaving us a little freer to talk during the 'astrology' session.

On the second week, I read Gillian's horoscope to find out how she was getting on with the basic leaflet design while waiting for the details from Maureen. It seemed she had lots of good ideas.

She was also full of suggestions for the Christmas-themed floats at the carnival, which everyone loved, especially Bill as he saw the event as a chance to sell lucrative hot pork rolls. Ian, the landlord, had enlisted a local band to play at the carnival, vouching that he'd just booked them for that date and not mentioned a word about the carnival. Janice showed me some historical notes she'd found to help put together ghost hunts, and Mick had talked to his head chef James about running festive cookery classes. He chuckled as he explained that he'd told James they would be a much-needed money-spinner for the restaurant rather than mentioning the campaign. I was pleased, both by everyone's enthusiasm and action but also with their understanding of the need to keep schtum.

By the time they left, my head was spinning with dates, times, and numbers, so I helped Rosie into the bath, read her a very quick bedtime story then sat and worked everything out for a little while. When I looked up from my work, I realised it had gone dark outside; it was past 10 o'clock. I looked around me and could hardly believe I'd invited people into my home when it looked such a state. I had to be up early for work the next morning but I felt compelled to clean at least part of the cottage before the start of the new week. As I swept out the hall and kitchen, I thought about how fond I was of Barbara, Bill, Mr Morris, all the folk who had got involved in the campaign. I still couldn't quite work Gillian out, but I felt her heart was in the right place. I smiled and remembered what my mother always told me: you can't judge a book by its cover. She also used to say a stranger would visit if you swept out after dark. I laughed at her old wives' tales, and realised how much I missed her and how very alone I felt at times. I had Rosemary, of course, but sometimes I missed having someone to call on for adult advice, even just adult conversation.

The floors swept, I closed and locked the door then made myself a cup of hot chocolate and settled down in front of the fire with my book. I knew I needed some escape from the campaign; I couldn't have that and fruit and vegetables taking over my life completely.

I awoke to Rosie tugging at my arm. I had fallen asleep and slept right through the night in the armchair.

'Gosh, Rosie, what time is it?' I said, with a start.

'It's nearly 8 o'clock, Mummy. I'm going to be late for school if you don't get a move on.'

'All right, sweetie, you go and get yourself washed and dressed. We'll have to eat breakfast on the way.'

I spent all my evenings that week baking bread and cakes ready for next yoga class. I knew I needed to muster as much determination as I could so I cooked tomato and basil tarts to stimulate our imaginations, together with cherry cakes because I knew they were difficult to resist. I also potted sprigs of rosemary in pretty pink-painted flowerpots for each individual to take home with them as a symbol of friendship. I hoped they would be a gentle daily reminder for the kitchen windowsill of the importance of always remembering our end goal.

Finally, one day on the way to work, I spotted the sign stuck up on the church notice board as promised. I chuckled to myself in delight when I saw it. I knew it had been a good idea to get Mrs Donaldson involved. She'd clearly whipped Maureen and Janice into shape with the research, giving Gillian just enough time to finish the design of the leaflets and posters before the Sullivans' anniversary. I hoped they'd found plenty of really interesting material which would enable us to take Ivory Meadows back to its former glory.

We continued our weekly 'exercise classes' and everything seemed to be going to plan. Fortunately Mr Johnson didn't turn up again, and Mr Baker soon nodded off during the relaxation session of our yoga workout. But we continued our 'astrology readings' just in any case he was only pretending. Jeremy, the choirmaster, had begun carol concert practice early for the choir, just saying he wanted it to be extra special this year and not revealing the real reason why. George, the bargee, had even bought himself a Santa suit and promised to play 'the big man' on both boat and steam train rides for the children. I'd been and had a word with Mrs Jacobs, the headmistress of Rosie's primary school, who had duly come along to our meeting and reported she had got the children making Christmas decorations and costumes early this year but without telling them they were to be part of the carnival parade. It was good to have her onside.

In mystical code, I told Janice that 'her inner thoughts were being heard loud and clear by those she didn't trust' – in other words to stop talking about the campaign outside these four walls. It was an indirect message to everyone, and they all nodded in mystical agreement.

At lunchtime on October 13, as promised, Dennis went to collect flowers from Gillian and brought them back to the shop. We could barely contain our excitement when we unwrapped the roses and discovered Gillian's beautiful posters and leaflets, carefully wrapped in clear plastic to protect them from getting damp. They were exquisite.

One read: 'Get ready for Christmas the Old-Fashioned Way. Come to a Christmas Carnival on December 1 in the pretty Georgian town of Ivory Meadows.' It went on to list all that would be on offer that day – a festive market offering handmade gifts, a travelling circus (Jeremy's idea), a procession of Christmas floats, a choir concert, yuletide food and drink and more.

Another read: "Get ready for Christmas the Old-Fashioned Way with a month-long calendar of festive events in the pretty Georgian town of Ivory Meadows throughout December." This one listed festive cookery courses, Christmas markets, ghost hunts, Santa riverboat trips, gift-making workshops, grand yuletide feasts, live music, carol concerts and more. There was a similar leaflet to accompany each poster, bearing more information and maps. Gillian really did have a talent. They looked hard to resist.

Closing the shop, I bid Barbara and Dennis, 'Happy Anniversary' and walked as fast as I could to get a train to the printers, Gillian's precious artwork concealed in my bag of library books. The staff at the printers were suitably discreet and, on my way home, I was able to hang my 'Lost Cat' sign on the old oak tree, with the number three as the last digit of the telephone number.

Three days later, Bill, George, and Jeremy the choirmaster did their work, taking collection of our contraband goods and carefully stashing them away from watchful eyes.

Bill blundered his way through the meeting that followed, nearly slipping up on exactly what he and the others had done until I solemnly told him it was Jeremy's turn to tell us his news. Jeremy was far more articulate when it came to talking in code. He told of how he had managed to book the travelling circus he'd mentioned, and that they were going to perform street acts around the town throughout the carnival. It sounded wonderful.

Gillian looked distressed though, saying she would help me make the tea and whispering to me she had made a potentially fatal flaw by holding on to one of her draft leaflets. It seemed she was rather fond of it, even though everyone had been told under no circumstances to keep any written matter in their homes and workplaces. She had carelessly left the precious draft lying around in her shop one day when the vicar had called in to pick up some flowers for his wife. Gillian assured me she'd whisked it away in time but I was a little unnerved and dished out some stern 'astrological' warnings to the others before they left, just to be certain.

I didn't mention that Mr Johnson had challenged me in the street, and that his parting shot had concerned me ever since: 'Your conundrums, Vivian, be sure they do puzzle me but they do not alarm me.'

52

Chapter Five

At last it was the weekend and we felt we could relax. I was happily cooking when Rosie came tiptoeing into the kitchen.

'Look, Mummy, I caught a ladybird,' she said.

'You caught a ladybird? You can't catch a ladybird, they catch you.' I smiled and wiped a smudge of dirt from her nose.

Together we sang: 'Ladybird, ladybird fly away home, your house is on fire and your children are alone' laughing as the ladybird opened its bright red wings and flew back into the garden. It was an old rhyme my mother used to sing to me to bring luck. She always said it made her feel happy when she sang it, even though the words weren't particularly kind. We spent the rest of the weekend chatting, reading, and baking together. It felt so good to have some time to ourselves. Rosie was growing into a very lovely, very caring girl.

I always loved the autumn, when the nights draw in and the trees seem to burn up in magnificent golds and brilliant reds. Barbara and I had been watching the weather from our cosy shop window all Monday afternoon, and it was on her insistence that I borrowed an umbrella to make my way home even though I had a day off the following day and so couldn't return it. I collected Rosie from school and, back at the cottage, she was full of the news of the day, telling me every last snippet in animated detail. It tired me out just watching her endless energy.

Rosie was hungry for fresh air and, after a light tea of

cherry jam sandwiches and cups of milky tea, the dark clouds seemed to clear so I allowed her to play in the garden for half an hour before bed. It gave me a little time to go over my schedule for the coming weeks. I had to write press releases to send to the local press. I was so engrossed in my work that Rosie made me jump when she came bounding into the kitchen, with Whisper the cat at her heel.

'We've discovered hidden treasure,' said Rosie. She marched triumphantly round the kitchen, saluted me and the cat, then placed a silver amulet on the table in front of us. It was covered in dirt but nonetheless it gleamed and sparkled as it caught the light.

'Where did you get this?' I asked.

'It was buried in the garden. Whisper and me, we were playing pirates and he led me straight to it. He just started digging so I joined in. We didn't have to dig deep to discover our treasure.'

There is an old myth that black cats are able to sniff out buried treasure, even so our little Whisper had surprised me.

'It is beautiful, darling,' I said to Rosie, wiping it with a cloth until its jewels started to shine, speckling the walls with emerald and sapphire as it caught the setting sun through the window.

Grabbing my hand, Rosie led me deep into the garden. There was still a heaviness to the air. The amulet in my hand seemed to shimmer even more in the stillness of the last rays of daylight. Rosie, joined by the cat again, led me to a small patch of earth they had dug up.

'See if you can find treasure too, Mummy?' Rosie egged me on.

I had to admit it was tempting to see if any other jewels lay further down the hole she'd made with her muddy hands. I fetched the shovel and dug a little deeper. Almost instantly I hit something hard. Carefully I used my hands to scrape away the dirt.

'What is it, Mummy?'

The 'treasure' came up easily from the ground, and I pulled it up for a closer inspection.

It was a skull. A miniature human skull. It must have been a child. I shuddered.

'Cool,' said Rosie, reaching out to touch it.

I slapped her hand, and quickly returned the skull to where I'd found it.

'Don't you want to see if the rest of the skeleton is there, Mummy?'

I felt my blood run cold, and knew I had to think fast. Should I call the police? No, it was probably best not to interfere. The skull looked old and discoloured, as if it had been buried long ago.

'Rosie, sometimes treasure is buried for a reason. If that's the case then under no circumstances should it be disturbed. What we've just found is important and special. But it must only be seen and known about by us two. We were privileged to have been led to it. Now we must not take advantage of that by telling others. Do you understand? You're not to tell anyone at school about this. It's our little secret.'

Rosie nodded solemnly: 'Like where we came from?'

'Yes, like where we came from.'

'And my daddy?'

'Yes, and Daddy. Run in now and wash and brush your teeth. Scrub that dirt from under your fingernails. It's time for your bed.'

'When will we see Daddy again?'

'Inside now, Rosie,' I said, sternly, 'it's late and getting dark. Do as you are told at once.'

Obediently she did as I asked, although I heard her grumbling as she made her way back into the house.

As dusk fell around me, I looked down at the tiny skull again and wept. It felt like the salty water of my tears opened up an enormous void inside my chest that had been closed for so long. I wept for the mother of this baby, who had been forced to lay her to rest at such a young age. I wept for the baby, who had all her life ahead of her but had been cruelly taken away. I wept at what this revelation might mean to me and Rosie. Why was this in our garden? Why had the cat led us here? Was there something larger than that that had led us to Cherrystone Cottage, to Ivory Meadows in the first place? Would we ever get to return to London, to see our old friends again?

I gently replaced the skull in the shallow grave where I had found it, covering it with earth once more. I put the silver trinket back into its rightful place, too. Then I cut some roses and placed them on top. At this, the cat leapt up and stood proudly amongst the flowers on top of the shrine. His eyes seemed to stare past me, deep into my soul. He seemed to be searching for something, something inside me that was too terrifying to be let out. He reminded me of a picture in an old storybook my mother used to read to me at night. It was about a cat which stood on top of a tombstone of a deceased woman whose soul had been possessed by the devil. My mother and her stories.

By the time I stood up, it had gone quite dark around me. There was not a star in the sky and the moon was surrounded by an eerie mist. I ran back up to the house, and slammed the door shut behind me. My head, which had been aching all day, was now pounding.

It wasn't just that something wasn't quite right. It was definitely that something was very wrong.

The kettle hissed on the stove. Perhaps Rosie's fairies weren't all good after all.

That evening, Rosie continued to ask too many questions, questions to which I had no answers. After she'd finally, grumpily, gone to bed, I paced up and down the kitchen, worrying about our gruesome discovery and the effect it had had on us both. Perhaps I would go to the police in the morning after all, although the thought filled me with dread.

Suddenly the entire room lit up as an almighty flash shot through the curtains. It was rapidly followed by an enormous roar of thunder that echoed and rolled around the house. Then the heavens opened and the rain poured so heavily on the roof it sounded like it might fall in. Still it was a relief to feel the heavy haze in my head clear now that the storm was finally here. I've always loved watching a storm pass. There's something hugely comforting about being tucked up safe and cosy indoors while Mother Nature provides the world's greatest theatre.

Going up to my bedroom, I sat on the window seat, transfixed by the spectacle of light and sound before me, together with the humming of the steady rain. The sky seemed to take on a warm, amber glow. It was strange and haunting in the coolness of the downpour. I opened the window; I wanted to feel the rain on my hands. Almost as quickly as it had started, the rain stopped and the intervals between the lightning and thunder grew longer. The storm was passing but the glow over the town was getting brighter. I breathed in the damp freshness and smelt ... fire.

Throwing on my raincoat and wellingtons, I gently roused Rosemary from her sleep, put on her coat and boots and carried her out of the house to raise the alarm.

By the time we reached Mr Morris's house, where I knew there was a telephone, there were sirens and bells in the town. Help was already on its way so we carried on down into the high street. By this time Rosie was wide awake and running as she clutched my hand.

It was Mr Shaw's house. The elderly postmaster's beautiful black-and-white timber home was ablaze. Flames were soaring out from the roof and the windows had blown out.

Then to our horror, we realised there was a ladder up to the bedroom window. Mr Shaw was trapped.

By now, quite a crowd had gathered and the men of the town were helping the firemen dump their hoses into the river. It seemed incredible that the riverside home that had previously been plagued with flooding was now on fire.

We edged closer to the house, shielding our faces from the burning heat and the dazzling brightness. I could hear a fireman shouting to Mr Shaw that he had to go. But Mr Shaw wouldn't go, not without his beloved dog, Jake. He loved that dog too dearly to leave him behind in the fire. I had never, ever seen the two of them apart.

There was a spine-chilling crack, and one of the roof joists began to give way. The chief fireman bravely pushed past the others and climbed in through the upstairs window. A hushed lull passed over the town. For what seemed an eternity, nobody moved. Apart from the crackle and hiss of the flames, you could have heard a pin drop in Ivory Meadows.

Then at last, the chief fireman appeared with Mr Shaw over his shoulder. He turned and carefully made his way back down the ladder, his feet barely touching the ground before the entire roof fell in. Mr Shaw was unconscious and it was clear his beloved little Jake was not with him.

The rest of the firemen gained control of the fire, pumping gallons of the life-giving river over the roofless, dead house. As Mr Shaw and the fire chief were taken to hospital by ambulance, the last of the flames died down and all that was left was a blackened, wooden carcass.

Choking fumes filled the air, and the firemen told everyone to go home and close their doors and windows. I wanted to get Rosie away from this hell before us. As we slowly made our way back up the hill, I was filled with grief for Mr Shaw. How would I feel if my beautiful Rosemary and our lovely, nurturing home were taken away from me in one sudden blow?

It was not until the next day that I realised the true significance of what had happened the night before. Mr Shaw's house had been the first property earmarked for demolition. He had told me, one time when he came into the shop to buy apples, that he had been offered vastly inflated figures to sell up and move out by the property developers. He said they had wanted to knock his home down to make way for a block of six luxury apartments called 'River View Estate'. But he had flatly refused each and every offer. He had grown up in that house, as had his father; he was not about to turn it over to a complete stranger to be bulldozed. So he had dug his heels in and stayed put. Now he was left with nothing. My mind raced. Could it be possible this wretched disaster was more than a tragic accident? I decided not to bother the police with my skeleton in the garden as they already had enough to deal with following the fire.

I talked to Barbara about my conspiracy theory as soon as I arrived at work the following day. It seemed just too awful to be the right conclusion. Barbara told me she and Dennis had been in the pub last night as they often stopped by for a quick drink after closing up the shop. Apparently by the time they reached The Mason Arms it was already a buzz with conspiracy theories on how the fire had started and who, if anyone, was to blame.

'All I kept thinking,' she said, 'was poor Mr Shaw and how lucky he had been to escape. It will, of course, break his heart that his faithful dog didn't make it out with him. Think that's the only thing he lived for, that dog. The firemen didn't realise that by saving Mr Shaw and not his dog that both would reach an early grave. Well, I know it's an awful thing to say, Vivian, and let's hope to God I'm wrong, but I don't think that man will last 'til Christmas.'

'Well, we need to keep a very close eye on him then, Barbara.'

'Yes, love, you're right. No one else'll bother though, mind. They were all too busy talking about the fire itself.'

'So what do you think caused it? Do you think it was the lightning?' I asked.

She looked away, busying herself, stacking the apples in baskets along the shelves: Golden Delicous, next to the Braeburn, next to the Jonagold, next to the Pink Ladies.

'What have they been saying, Barbara?'

'Oh nothing, love. Could you pass me the Granny Smiths from that carton over there, please?'

Taking the box over, I put my hand on her arm and said, 'I would much sooner know the truth, Barbara, honestly. If you're a friend you'd tell me.'

'All right, love. Now you know I don't agree with this and neither does Bill. That's what's got him into so much trouble.'

'Bill's in trouble?' I exclaimed. Had Bill started the fire? Surely not. 'What on earth's been going on?'

'Let's sit down, love. I'll tell you what happened from the beginning but you must promise me you won't get excited and do anything rash.'

'Go on,' I said.

She took a deep breath. 'Everyone was just chattering away madly when we arrived at the pub last night, must have been around ten-ish after we'd packed everything away and locked up, what with being delayed by watching the fire.

'Then over the general din, I heard two voices more animated than anyone else.

'I looked over – as did everyone – it was Mr Johnson and Bill. The mayor was saying, 'It's a natural demolition this, how lightning had struck the timber building and it was nature's way of choosing who and what survives. That's nature's way, isn't it? Survival of the fittest.'

'Bill shouted back that it was claptrap and that the mayor was only saying it because it suited his own evil scheme.

'The mayor replied, and I remember this clearly, '*My
evil scheme, my boy?*' He went onto reveal for the first
time why he had come to Ivory Meadows. I must say we
were all naturally intrigued.

'It turned out, a couple of years ago, Bill had dropped
into an out-of-town pub one evening after making some
deliveries. He had taken solace in drink and a stranger's
ear, revealing how business was bad because the younger
folk were using the supermarkets and the older generation,
his only loyal customers, were dying out.

'Unfortunately the man sat next to the stranger was the
man who would go on to become our mayor. The seed was
planted in his mind, it didn't require a criminal
mastermind to bring it to fruition. He and his brother – a
major property developer – decided the best way to bring
about change was by winning people's trust and, to do
that, he would have to become their mayor.

'It seems the project, which the mayor now believes to
be unstoppable, will make him and his brother
millionaires.

'Bill, as you can imagine, was incensed both at the
mayor and himself. He felt he was to blame and had to do
something about it.

'Meanwhile, Mr Johnson carried on relentlessly. He
was clearly enjoying himself. He said, "The fire was God's
way of telling you lot that these old buildings have had
their day. They're crumbling round the edges and a terrible
fire hazard, as we've just seen. Why, I'll bet that one was
hardly fit for human occupation."

'Bill piped up, "I can't believe what you're saying.
What about poor Mr Shaw? You saying he deserved to
lose his home and dog?"

'The mayor shook his head.'

Barbara contorted her face and I could see how the
weasel of a man had been enjoying every moment of the

whole wretched showdown.

She continued, 'The mayor said, "Someone else decided his fate for him, I'm afraid. And if it wasn't God then it had to be the work of the devil."

'Well, a hushed tremor ran round the room. Though they'd never admit it to your face, Vivian, this community is an old-fashioned lot. They like to pretend they're modern and up with the times but they still believe in idle gossip and old wives' tales. And just the word Lucifer, God bless us all,' she said, crossing her heart, 'well, you understand, it's enough to upset even the strongest of dispositions.'

'What are you talking about, Barbara?' I asked. I didn't quite follow where all this had come from.

'Bill asked the same thing, love, only rather more aggressively. The mayor smiled. It was obvious he was enjoying it, the horrible fox of a man. He said, "You can't tell me for one moment, young fellow, that you haven't noticed a change in Ivory Meadows in the past couple of months? I can't see that it's the climate or the landscape that's changed but ..."' Barbara paused.

'Go on,' I urged her.

'He said, "More a new arrival on the hill."'

'He's always hated me,' I said, 'I'm not surprised, but don't worry, he doesn't scare me.'

'No, love, I don't think you quite understand what he meant. Bill grunted at him, "If you mean Miss Myrtle then the only change she's brought to the town is a good one."' Lots of people nodded and mumbled their agreement.'

I couldn't help but smile. It was nice to hear my efforts, however small, were appreciated.

'But,' said Barbara, 'the mayor continued, "You think the fact Peter's cattle caught a disease and had to be destroyed is a positive sign? And the fact most of Mr Parson's orchard turned out to be rotten just a co-incidence? And the fact less and less people are bothering to get out of their beds and turn up to church on a Sunday, I suppose that's just modern-day idleness, is it? And the fact half the town got food poisoning from the lamb you bought in from the farm just up from Cherrystone Cottage?"

'Bill said, 'Now steady on, I apologised for that and promised I'd never use Bidcup's meats again. All my meat has been perfect ever since. Has it not?' he said, looking round. People nodded but you could see the seed of doubt had been sewn.

'"And this fire," the mayor carried on like some awful circus master, enthralling the crowd, "fires don't just start by themselves, do they?"

'A gasp went round the room, Vivian, I'll tell you. The mayor continued, relentlessly, like a dog with a bone, only now probably for the first time since learning of his ulterior motive, people actually wanted to listen to what he had to say. They were intrigued. He said, "She spends all her days pretending to be a normal greengrocer's assistant. Then, at night, she's cooped up all alone in that tatty old cottage with just her daughter. We all know she spends too much time with that old battleaxe, Miss Metford. It's not right, a woman of her age, to be without a husband. Who knows what she does there? I know she holds astrology classes, filling people's minds with mumbo-jumbo, and she grows plants and herbs for spells."'

'Poppycock,' I interrupted, 'everyone else, bar Johnson and the vicar, know exactly what those classes are and that they're nothing to do with astrology.'

'Yes, I know, dear, and I thought the same but what he said made it worse. He said, "Those classes she holds up at her house, don't you realise they're not astrology? She's brainwashing each and every one of you so that when she cast a spell that would burn Mr Shaw's house to the ground nobody would think it was her, would they? No one but the only two people who haven't been brainwashed – myself and the vicar."

'These were his words: "She's pure evil, the vicar has seen it, I've seen it, but you've all been too blind to see for yourselves."'

I was speechless, gasping for breath with tears welling in my eyes.

Barbara kindly touched my hand and stroked my face the way my mother used to. She nodded at me and tilted her head just enough to show me she didn't believe the wicked words of the mayor.

'Get the poor girl a glass of water, will you, Dennis? I'm afraid there's worse to come yet, dear. Brace yourself.'

Worse yet? What could be worse than rumours being spread that I was a witch? In an old-fashioned town like this, they'd drown a woman for less. I gulped the water, took a deep breath and asked Barbara to tell me what happened next.

'It was Bill. He was enraged. You see, I don't know if you've ever noticed it, you've been so busy with the campaign and Rosie, of course. But since the day you first arrived, he's always had a soft spot for you.'

I blushed, I couldn't help it. I had no idea. How could I have been so blind? I guess I'd just shut out all thoughts of advances from men.

'He couldn't bear to hear such things being said about you. He slowly got up out of his seat and walked over to Johnson. The mayor had turned and was brashly asking who was going to buy him a drink. He didn't see Bill approach. Before we knew it Bill had punched him with such force, he knocked him clean off his feet.

'At first people applauded and cheered. But then Johnson didn't get up. They waited, some people shouted at him to stop being such a drama queen, but there was no movement whatsoever. He was out cold, unconscious, and blood was streaming rapidly from his head where he'd hit the bar on the way down.

'I jumped up. I knew however much I hated him, someone had to do something. Bill had punched him on the back of his neck. Had the mayor been facing the other way it might not have been so drastic. Bill didn't know he'd hit the weakest part of the skull. I remembered that from the First Aid training I'd done as a girl.

'Johnson was still out cold and the blood was getting worse. It had saturated the pub carpet, turning it from light green to putrid brown. I looked around me. Everyone was rooted to the spot. Bill had already fled in a rage. I doubt he had any idea just how seriously he'd injured the mayor. People were whispering "Is he dead?"

'I checked for a pulse. It was still there. Just. I screamed for an ambulance and, as if lifted from a trance, they all sprang to action. It was sheer chaos. Everyone on top of each other, and Ian, the landlord, trying to calm everyone down, reassuring them the ambulance was already on its way.

'It seemed to take forever for the paramedics to arrive. But I suppose it was really only five or ten minutes. They checked his pulse, lifted him onto a stretcher, and hurried him off to hospital.

'Back in the pub, it was like the calm after the storm. Everyone returned to their tables and drank silently. It was like everyone knew this one small but almighty act had changed the town, changed it forever. They were clearly weighing up who was right, who was wrong, and, I'm sorry to say, whether there was any truth in the mayor's vicious rumours. You see, if there was, then that meant everything they believed in, everything they were fighting for, was wicked, cruel, and unjust.

'You see you, me, and Bill, we know Johnson's game, we know there's no witchcraft behind the magic you create up at that little cottage. Don't stop me, Vivian, you know yourself there's something magical about what you're doing, what you've achieved. But the rest of the town –

they're an old-fashioned, God-fearing lot – even the mere suggestion of devil-worshipping and they'll turn and run a mile.'

My mind drifted back to Miss Metford. Those were the exact words she'd used when she'd warned me to be careful last time I saw her.

'And the insinuation that they themselves have been following a cult,' Barbara continued, 'frankly it doesn't bear thinking what reaction they might have.'

'And what about Bill?' I asked, drifting back into reality.

'Ah, Bill. I was just coming to him. The police went straight round to his house. They arrested him late last night and he's been locked up in a cell ever since. People are saying Mr Johnson is in a coma. Everyone who was at the pub has been questioned and I expect you'll receive a visit later today. They're waiting to see what happens to the mayor as to whether they charge Bill for murder or attempted murder.'

'Dear God,' I said, throwing my head into my hands. This was all too much. Not only was Mr Shaw's house a charred shell and his dog dead, now a man lay in a coma, Bill was being branded a murderer, and I was in the middle of a witch hunt. I felt horribly responsible for everything that had happened. Much as I hated Johnson, I would never have wished him dead.

I hadn't realised I was crying. Great big tears were rolling down my cheeks, causing a well of salt on my blouse.

'There, there,' comforted Barbara, 'I'm so sorry to upset you but I felt you ought to know.'

'I'm grateful that you did. It's all my fault; how could I have been so stupid? I must go and visit Bill and, of course, Mr Johnson in hospital.'

'You'll do no such thing, young lady. You mustn't go anywhere near Bill. You could make his case much worse, and you could even go down with him. You need to lay low for there's one more thing I have left to tell you.'

'Not more,' I cried. I didn't think my heart could take any more.

'Be strong for me for one more moment, Vivian,' she said, clutching my hands in hers. 'I have to tell you this for your own good. Somehow the press has got hold of the story.'

With this, she revealed the front page of *The Herald*. It read: 'Butcher Bloodbath – Allegations of Witchcraft Following Attack on Town Mayor .'

'How did they hear about this?' I asked, bewildered. 'Why are they interested in a little pub brawl in Ivory Meadows?'

'You have to see, love, they're blowing the whole thing out of proportion. It reads lower down that they've had an anonymous tip-off. It could be anyone but it strikes me there's only one man, who's not in a coma, that would want to spread this evil gossip about the town. That's God's own preacher. It means, Viv love, that you must be very careful who you talk to. Mention some triviality to a stranger and it'll end up as hocus-pocus in the papers. Do you understand what I'm saying to you?'

I nodded.

'And it would do you no harm to keep away from Miss Metford. Whether she's a hermit, an eccentric, or a witch doesn't matter to most people. All they see her as is trouble. I'm just saying, if you don't want your finger burnt, don't play with fire.

'Now, Dennis is going to walk you home. Take this box of groceries with you, and lock yourself in. Don't come out until things have calmed down a bit, I'll come and visit you in the morning.'

I picked up my coat and hat to go, and Dennis steadied me with his hand.

'Oh, and remember, don't go opening your door to any

strangers.'

We fetched Rosemary from school early then walked blindly into the bitingly cold air. It stung my face where I had been crying. The police were on their way to my house. What on earth could I tell them about this, and about my own skeletons?

Chapter Six

The police were with me within half an hour of my returning home. I sent Rosie to play in her bedroom with Whisper while I made the officers a cup of tea, my head swimming as the kettle boiled.

Fortunately they said the mayor was fine. He hadn't been in a coma at all, it was just that the scandal had grown way out of proportion through word of mouth. Bill had been released but the mayor was pressing charges.

I told them my version of events, how I wasn't there and didn't know what they were talking about with regards to strange meetings. I told them I realised yoga was a little new-age for Ivory Meadows but that I felt the locals could cope with it. They chuckled so I brought out the cake tin and, encouraged, began to chat to them about how good it is for your health and how they should try it.

The female officer did ask why had I come to Ivory Meadows and where I had come from, which almost made me choke on my cake crumbs, but I explained I'd been made redundant from my last job in the city and that, as a single mum, I decided it was time for a new start for Rosie and myself in the country. I then began rambling about fresh air and wholesome food and we were soon well off the subject.

They finally left, bellies full of cake and tea, and happy that the whole debacle had been a silly misunderstanding.

I sank down onto the floor behind the door as soon as I'd closed it. The last thing I wanted was for the police to go digging into my past. I didn't mention the skeleton and

I laughed off any amorous feelings I might have for Bill. After all that was ridiculous, the last thing I needed in my life right now was a man, even though I was touched he had stuck up for me.

The next knock at the door was a journalist. Fortunately I asked who was there and refused to open the door so they weren't able to get a picture of my face. After all these months of hiding, I would certainly be discovered if my picture was in the local rag. After many attempts at persuasion, the reporter finally went away. Thank goodness no one in the town had ever taken a photograph of me, otherwise my face would have surely graced the pages of the newspaper.

I couldn't believe I'd left myself and Rosie so exposed to discovery and vowed to keep my head down from that point on. At the end of the day, it was our lives I was trying to protect, not the rest of the town.

I spent the next three days moping around the cottage. No one from Ivory Meadows came to see me, and I couldn't help but feel I was perhaps just making the situation worse for myself by steering clear of the community. As far as I was concerned I had nothing to hide but I knew my absence would be viewed as an admission of guilt.

I had not given Rosie the full details of why I was at home, and keeping her off school. I told her I was feeling sick and didn't want to see anyone. She was delighted as it meant we had more time to spend together. But somehow I really didn't feel like playing games, dancing, and laughing like we normally did. Fortunately, Rosie's previous interrogation had now ceased and she was back to being my lovely, caring daughter again, doing all she could, once again, to look after her mum and make her feel better.

I kept myself locked away during daylight hours, only stepping out in the cool crisp moonlit nights for a breath of fresh air, and to try to come to terms with the gravity of my situation. I barely slept in any case. Tonight, outside in the cold night air, an eldritch light glowed all over the cottage, illuminating its white-washed walls. I looked up to see the moon but the sky was dark and hazy. The light seemed to come from something else, something strange and unearthly. It made the trees look like eerie figures, with long spindly fingers outstretched over the house. Were they protecting or attacking us?

I rebuked myself for getting caught up in Miss Metford's meddlesome delusions. Surely it was just my eyes playing tricks with me.

Or was Miss Metford, and indeed the mayor, right after all? No, that was just a drunken, crazy night, and to be honest I'd been quite flattered by the fact she thought me capable of magic. It felt nice to be a 'couple of silly old witches' but I only went along with it because it felt good to be part of a team again. The reality was that what she had said was nonsense. For all that I rather liked Miss Metford's robust eccentricity, I couldn't help but feel it wouldn't do Rosie or me good to spend much time with her now.

I looked back up again and the cottage and the gruesome trees had gone back to normal once more. Rosie was staring down at me from the upstairs window. Her pale face looked doll-like with her golden hair tied back behind her head. It looked as though she'd stepped into an ancient sepia photograph. Unnerved, I ran back indoors to check on her.

I was upset. I didn't know what to do with myself. I was afraid to even cook anything as my mother had always told me only to cook when you feel happy because your mood will always come through the food. I'd tried making an egg mayonnaise sandwich but, without thinking, undercooked the eggs and their yolks had spilled everywhere. I sat with my head in my hands. I was crying over spilled eggs and there was nothing I could do to stop. Maybe I should have stayed in London and gone back to my old job in PR. At least there I was successful; I was wanted.

There was a knock at the door. It made me jump. No one had ventured near me since the day I'd retreated home. I was all of a panic, not knowing what to do. Before I'd even had the chance to work out my actions, the door was opened and Miss Metford flounced in.

'Hello, Viv dear, thought you might need a little tot of gin and some pigeon pie,' she said, waving a bottle in front of my face.

'Oh, it's you,' I said, both relieved that it wasn't the press, police, or vicar but frustrated as I no longer wanted to associate myself with the old witch on the hill; it had caused me enough trouble as it was. How had I been so careless as to leave the door unlocked?

'Well that's nice,' she said, plonking herself down on a chair next to me and lighting a cigarette. 'I go to all this trouble cooking, I don't normally cook you know, and that's the thanks I get.

'Don't try to interrupt me, Vivian. I know you've been advised to stay away from me, but I've been watching you and frankly I think you could do with a friend. And a decent supper.'

At this, she pulled a dead bird out of her bag and emptied the rest of the contents onto the work surface. Just at that moment, Rosie raced into the kitchen, coming to an abrupt halt as soon as she saw what Miss Metford was proposing for dinner.

'You're surely not going to cook that here, are you?' I asked, barely believing my eyes.

'You try to stop me, young lady. My father always used to make pigeon pie for us when times were hard. I've even dug out his old recipe to follow. Now let me see, "pluck, singe and draw the pigeon".'

'Cool,' said Rosie, a look of sheer awe and amazement in her eyes as she watched Mary begin to prepare the bird. The two of them had started to become close over the last few weeks and it seemed a shame to deprive my daughter of a little fun. She'd had to put up with living with a grumpy mum in isolation for too long.

And I knew Mary was right, I did need a friend.

Despite Rosie's many questions and Mary's rather over-indulgent explanations, I still had to turn away as feathers flew everywhere in the kitchen.

'Let's see,' Mary continued, 'he doesn't look too bad, does he, Viv?' she said, shoving a scrawny, bald bird under my face.

'Shot him on my way down to you so he's as fresh as morning dew. Right, now "wash under cold running water". Think I can manage that, eh, Viv? Especially as you don't have any hot.'

It was a problem at the cottage I'd been meaning to sort out for weeks.

'Now, "remove flesh". Where's your cleaver?'

'I don't have one I'm afraid, Mary.'

'I'll have to make do with a normal knife then. Good job I'm a strong old bird myself, eh?'

Eventually, I turned and watched as she struggled with the poor, decapitated pigeon. Somehow I no longer felt like eating.

'Right, think that's done it.' There was a miniscule amount of meat left on the chopping board. I had to smile.

'Just going to boil him up now for twenty minutes while I make the pastry. Where's your flour?'

I pointed her in the right direction and within no time the place was covered in white dust, as if it had been left untouched for centuries. Rosie looked like a little street urchin and Mary herself looked as white as a shrouded woman. I had to laugh. It felt good; it was the first time I'd laughed in almost a week.

'Would you like some help, Mary?'

'No, I'm quite capable, thank you, dear. I have cooked in my time, you know. Or at least I did once or twice.' She shot me one of her devilish grins. There was something irresistibly impudent about her.

'I think that pastry will do,' she said, trying to run the gloopy mixture between her fingers.

'Is that really how it's supposed to look?' Rosie mouthed to me across the kitchen.

I kept my lips sealed, trying desperately not to erupt into giggles with my daughter, who had her impish grin back again.

'I'll just dig out your casserole dish, here it is. And, as you can see, I've already taken the liberty of trimming some herbs out of your garden. Basil to stimulate your brain, stop you sitting here all weepy, and coriander to beat your apathy. I want to see a bit more vigour in you, girl.

'Sprinkle those on the top with a little of the pigeon stock. Cover with pastry, ummn, like so, and pop him in the oven. There, easy. Now let's have a drink to our culinary success.' She poured two large gins. I fetched a glass of milk for Rosie.

'We haven't tried it yet,' I sheepishly told her.

'All the more reason for numbing the taste buds first, my dear,' she said, then cackled with laughter.

That was it, all three of us laughed until our sides felt sore. Well, not quite as sore as we were likely to feel after we'd eaten her ill-fated pigeon.

'You know,' said Miss Metford, as she poured another gin after 'dinner', 'I've also got one of father's recipes here for stewed eels.'

This time both Rosie and I screwed up our noses. From what we'd eaten so far, Mary's meals were clearly something of an acquired taste – and not one either of us

74

really banked on acquiring. That said, Rosie had tucked in wholeheartedly, I think simply because she didn't want to offend her dear, elderly friend.

Mary seemed not to notice and instead carried on in her usual oblivious fashion. 'They're quite a delicacy, you know and popular in years gone by in this area,' she told us.

'Father served them with mushrooms, parsley, onions, sherry, Worcestershire sauce, and lemon juice and he topped the whole thing off with slices of hard-boiled egg and pastry.'

'It does actually sound half decent, Mary, but after tonight, I think you should maybe put your culinary endeavours on hold again for another few years. No offence, of course.'

'None taken. Never liked cooking anyway,' she grunted, and we all laughed again.

Heartened by the previous night's meal, or perhaps looking for something a little more satisfying, Rosie went into the freezer the following morning and found a lamb casserole and cherry pie, which she defrosted and stuck in the oven for dinner. The smells of last summer drifted up the winding stairs and into my bedroom, where I had been taking a nap. It stirred all those feelings of love, warmth, and tenderness I'd felt both for Rosie and the town when I'd been baking frantically. Looking back I'd sensed then I was in for a hard winter but had been so caught up in the campaign and controversy, had failed to realise this was it. I wandered downstairs to find Rosie had laid our battered little kitchen table with a pretty rose-print cloth and had placed a bowl of fruit in the centre for decoration. Somehow the room felt warmer than it had done for days and, touched, I took the casserole out of the oven and began ladling big spoonfuls into our bowls. We ate in silence but towards the end I felt my cheeks beginning to burn with vitality and good health. Rosie just smiled her smile of pure sunshine. She seemed very much older than her years in so many ways.

As we tucked into the sweet but tart cherry pie, I let the juices dribble down my chin, remembering how they'd stained my hands red with the vigour of my cooking endeavours. It had been worthwhile after all. Suddenly Rosie yelped. She'd bitten her tongue by trying to eat too quickly. I touched her cheek and smilingly rebuked her, 'You must have recently told a lie.'

She looked at me solemnly, put down her spoon and said: 'Not me, Mummy, you.'

'What do you mean, Rosie?'

'Mummy, you haven't been honest with me about why you're off work and I'm off school. I know when you're sick because I can feel it in my tummy,' she said, patting her stomach, 'and the feeling I have now is much more in my throat. I think you're sad about something but you won't share it with me.'

I bowed my head in shame. How could I have been so foolish as to think I could hide something like this from a child as intuitive as my daughter?

'Rosie, I'll tell you the truth. The only reason I haven't before is that I wanted to try to protect you. I realise now I'm probably putting you in greater danger by not letting you know what's been going on.

'The truth is, love, well, it's …'

'Just tell me, Mummy, I'm not afraid. Is it about my daddy?'

Her daddy. I hadn't even considered him. Because I hadn't heard anything of him since the vicar first mentioned 'a strange man' months ago, I'd thought it was a fluke, or that perhaps Mr Baker was bluffing for his own benefit. For weeks I'd been watching my back, keeping my cards close to my chest in case he showed up.

But he hadn't, so I'd decided to turn a blind eye and

get on with my life. With Mary Metford onside, I felt I did have someone who might stand up to him for me if push came to shove. But now, everything had changed. I didn't feel so strong any more. If my face hit the newspapers he'd be sure to find us out and come and grab Rosie. I did, however, know Rosie was finding life difficult and confusing without her father around.

'No, Rosie, this has nothing to do with your father,' I said, trying to compose myself, ready to tell her the already devastating news I had.

'This is all to do with me. You see, although we've been here for a couple of months now, we're still seen as the new people in town. Some people, like Mr Shaw, whose house recently burnt down, some people like him have families who have been here for generations, for hundreds of years. They don't take kindly to new blood in the town. They think we'll disturb their ways.'

'But Mr Shaw has always been really nice,' interrupted Rosie.

'Mr Shaw was a bad example, he's just on my mind.'

I decided to take another tack, I was getting nowhere here. 'Rosie, some nasty rumours have been spread about Mummy. They have made some of the people here think I'm a … a bad person. These rumours are lies, just made up to try to stop me from doing what I feel is good and right for the town. There's no need for you to believe anything you hear. Do you understand me?'

'Not really, Mummy, but I'll let you know if anyone says anything bad. Can I go and play now with Whisper?'

'Of course you can, sweetheart,' I said, glad my cross-examination was over for today. Fortunately it had mattered more to Rosie for me to understand I couldn't fool her than for her to sit and listen to her mother complain. For once I was grateful.

It was time for me to leave my beloved little cottage and face the world again. The house itself felt like such a safety blanket, a barrier protecting us from the rest of the world and whatever horrors lay there. But I couldn't stay here forever. It was Halloween in a couple of days' time, and I couldn't risk any more rumours of witchcraft due to my absence. Lord only knew what the local people might think I was up to that night if they didn't see me out and about.

Besides, there was work to be done. There was only just over a month before we were due to start our old-fashioned Christmas festivities. Although I was scared, I knew I couldn't just let Mr Johnson and his brother destroy Ivory Meadows. In fact, the more I thought about it, the more I realised the likes of Barbara and Bill shouldn't just give up. I had no idea whether they had got any of the posters put up or leaflets delivered while I'd been holed up in Cherrystone Cottage. Either way, there was a town to save and, witch or no witch, I was going to make sure it was saved if it was the last thing I did. I needed to make something good; I *needed* to be able to save something good in my life, having lost so much already.

I knew I had a battle on my hands. After all, the bloodshed hitting the newspaper meant Ivory Meadows was no longer a town nobody had heard of but the place on everyone's lips. It was a disaster. As the mayor was still recovering I knew it would be in bad taste to try to rally people round again to fight against his plans, even though it was clear now they would go on with or without him, thanks to his brother.

I would just try to go back to normal. It was the only way I stood a chance of survival in this old-fashioned town. I was determined, but it was a terrifying prospect.

I returned to work the following Monday and was welcomed back with open arms by Barbara and Dennis. Barbara whispered that the posters were still in hiding and, just as I'd suspected, nothing had been done to further the campaign in my absence. We were busy for the rest of the day so I didn't have a chance to talk to her any further. I myself spent much of my time trying to fend off the suspicious looks that kept coming my way from the customers.

Glad it was the end of the day, I decided to pop round to see Bill on my way to fetch Rosie from school. I was touched by what he'd done for me, even if it was a little heavy-handed and had landed all of us in trouble. He was busy out the back of his shop, chopping meat, when I arrived. He had enlisted the help of Scott, Barbara's eldest son, who was running the front of the shop until, as Barbara said Bill put it, 'the stink died down'.

Even from behind, he looked different, more vulnerable somehow. Something about his hunched shoulders made me want to reach out and touch him. I didn't. Instead I called out his name gently and he spun round on the spot.

'Oh, Vivian, you made me jump,' he said, blushing.

'How are you, Bill?' I asked.

'I guess you've heard what happened? Don't like anyone speaking out of line about anyone, especially when it's the pantomime mayor,' he said, his features hardening as he retold his version of events.

'Blabbing on he was; someone had to stop him. I just hope I haven't put a spanner in the works for you and your campaign,' he said, looking me in the eye for the first time. He seemed like a little, lost puppy dog.

'Not at all, Bill,' I mumbled, embarrassed. I'd hoped we'd be able to simply brush off what had happened and carry on as before. Clearly that wasn't to be the case. Resolutely, I grabbed his hand.

'What you did for me was incredible, Bill. No one has ever stood up for me that way before. I came here today to say thank you.'

He held my gaze for a moment, and I was surprised to

feel a spark of electricity between us.

'Now I must go,' I said, 'it's time for me to collect Rosie from school. I'll see you around. Take care of yourself, Bill.' And with that I turned and fled. I tried to put all thoughts of Bill out of my mind. I couldn't possibly fall for him.

I still wasn't over Rosemary's father. He had been the love of my life. We'd met when we were young. He was in his final year of college when I joined as a naïve fresher. I thought he was a bit of a god. I'd never really believed in love at first sight, thinking it was the stuff of trashy romantic novels, but the chemistry between us was amazing. He had long red hair and eyes that I could sink into, like pools of water. They seem to dance, and to change colour from hazel to green in the light. He quickly became my knight in shining armour, rescuing me when my car broke down, if I got too tipsy on a night out with the girls, or if I needed help when I started my first job as an office junior.

We had a wonderful wedding, surrounded by all our friends and family, followed by an idyllic Tuscan honeymoon. We were both career-minded and driven, which meant we worked and played hard. Life was for living in our eyes, and we wanted to gobble up every last drop. I had made my way up the ladder to a successful senior role in public relations, handling big brand accounts. He had ventured into marketing, learnt the tricks of the trade from various small companies, and gone on to set up his own business. He loved it; we both did. It gave us a great deal of freedom.

When Rosemary came along, everything changed. Our reactions to our poorly little baby were so far apart it began to feel as though we existed in different stratospheres. We no longer had the same goals and dreams.

We both had blood on our hands.

Chapter Seven

Much to my relief Halloween passed without event and we weren't visited by any trick or treaters. I asked Rosie if everything was OK at school and she just shrugged her shoulders, saying it was a bit boring at the moment. I could take boring until the cows came home; that's what I yearned for: a nice quiet, peaceful, boring life. Barbara laughed when I said this to her at work and suggested I needed to get out more. She'd taken it upon herself to become a surrogate mother to me. She decided it wasn't healthy for me to be cooped up in my little crumbling cottage all the time and so insisted on babysitting the following Sunday so I could enjoy a walk on my own, to get a bit of fresh air, a bit of 'me-time', as she put it.

Rosie and I had walked together lots at the weekends up until a fortnight ago. Now there was something so liberating about the thought of getting out on my own. It would give me a chance to think about my past and piece together a future for Rosie and myself.

It was getting late when Barbara arrived on Sunday afternoon, cursing her son Charlie for leaving his school project until the last minute. I promised I'd just take a short walk. The chilly November nights were drawing in earlier with each day that passed and I didn't want to be out when it was too dark.

I'd left Rosie playing with Barbara and her toys upstairs in her bedroom. They had come to love their time together, Rosie seeing Barbara as something of a fun auntie. I knew Barbara sneaked a stash of chocolate into my house every time she came but I turned a blind eye. It was nice for Rosie to have an adult friend, someone who wasn't seven years' old and at her school. I knew she missed her own family but that was an inevitable peril when you went on the run. For our own safety, I had to keep her away from our old friends and family, no matter how painful that was for me, her, or them. I thought about the campaign and decided it was probably best to leave our lovely posters and leaflets in hiding. What a pity Gillian and everyone else had gone to so much effort for nothing.

I breathed a long deep sigh, taking in the crisp air and watching my breath linger on the wind in front of me before drifting off elsewhere. The deeper I walked into the forest, the louder the birds sang, high up in the tall fir trees. I loved the fact they gave us a beautiful dusk chorus, celebrating the end of every great day as well as the joy and gratitude they gave us every morning for sun-up. This afternoon it was almost as if they sang:

'It's dusk, it's dusk beware
Everything looks golden
But soon it will be dark
And something will give you a scare.'

I smiled. Wise little birds. I decided to walk only as far as the river today and not to cross the railway bridge over it and into the glade on the other side. In the summer, Rosie and I had enjoyed going over there on the rare sunny days there had been. We'd lie there looking up at the sky. It was calming to put my worries into perspective, seeing just how tiny I was compared to the great big world around me. We'd take it in turns suggesting which clouds looked like they were the shape of an animal or a train. Rosie's were usually the most fanciful; she often saw mermaids, dragons, unicorns, and other such mythical creatures. I loved her vivid imagination. Sometimes we'd just lie there in silence, making up stories in our heads or closing our eyes and listening to all the wondrous sounds of the meadow so different to the haunting noises in the forest. Here the birds chatted away and the squirrels scampered up and down the tall trees on the edge of the glade, hiding their stash for winter, the bees busily too-ing and fro-ing between the brightly coloured flowers.

Once, we lay there silently, only to open our eyes and see a deer, hovering unsure between two trees in the entrance to the woods. When she realised we'd seen her she took off, elegantly cantering back into her darkened den. More recently, we'd ventured over there, wrapped up in our coats, hats, and gloves. Snuggling up together under a tree, telling stories, we'd both drifted off. I opened my eyes to find the glade had gone quite dark around us, and the grass was illuminated by magnificent glow-worms. I had roused Rosie and she looked about her in wonder and delight. We felt the magic of the woods that night as it guided us back home safely, even though our eyes had become redundant in the black of the night.

But no, I had no fear of needing to steady my step here today because I'd be home long before it got too dark to see. And, in any case, I knew the paths like the back of my hand and could probably get back with my eyes closed.

As I approached the stream that led down to the river I could hear it gurgling and hissing and popping like a newly opened bottle of home-made lemonade being poured into a glass.

'Glip, glop, go away
Now is not the time to stay
Go, go far from here
If you don't it'll end in teeeaaaaaarrrrrss …'

I chuckled with the stream. I was so used to making up

songs for Rosie I heard them even when she wasn't with me.

'I'll have to remember that one for next time she's here with me,' I said, aloud. My voice sounded strange, loud and somehow alien amongst the undergrowth. It caused a flurry of birds to scatter out of the trees and soar into the air above me. I'd been part of the woods, barely noticeable to the wildlife, until I'd opened my mouth. My voice was the one thing that gave me away, it was so different to the voices of the singing birds, buzzing insects, whistling wind, creaking trees, and rustling leaves dancing around me. Now the whole forest stood still. I stood with it, silently watching and waiting, as it watched me, nervously working out if I was friend or foe.

It took a couple of minutes. A robin took to the stand. I strained my eyes to see him, not daring to move my head. I was the defendant. He, the judge, sat pompously puffing out his chest in a tall tree looking down on the rest of the forest. A wood pigeon bumbled a coo-coo and promptly fell out of his tree, flapping his wings to steady himself, blatantly pretending he meant to do it all along. The forest erupted into hysterics. The birds cackled away, some cawing, others cawing, and the blue tits snootily tutting in annoyance at the wood pigeon's stupidity. The squirrel scurried up and down the tree in excitement.

Finally the robin let out a beautiful rendition of his favourite song and the forest quietened down again. I thought for a moment I was going to get off lightly, thanks to the wood pigeon's decoy.

By now, the blackbirds had started to surround me in the twilight. I hadn't noticed them at first. Two stood next to me on the ground, which didn't seem too strange, considering they are such sociable little fellows. But, as I watched, another flew down to join his brothers, then another, then another until I was surrounded by blackbirds, like jailers ready and eager to take down the crook. I counted them, silently, nervously trying not to move. Seven. Seven's supposed to be lucky. Perhaps I would get away with my forest faux pas after all. And yet, in the dusk light there was something terribly eerie about these seemingly gentle birds.

The robin sang again. He'd jumped down a few branches of his tree and I could see him clearly now. It was as if he were walking down a set of vast courtroom steps to address the low life – myself – below. He was a very handsome chap with a pillar-box red chest, puffed out with pride. The forest hushed again. His song was beautiful, mesmerising. It sounded so exquisite I could hardly imagine he was passing a guilty verdict. I looked nervously at the blackbirds. They were slowly backing away, cursing the robin for his decision. The great tits were chirping 'well done' while their fellow blue tits were shrugging their shoulders, as if to mutter 'what had the drama been all about?' and urging everyone to carry on their business as if nothing had happened.

I did feel guilty. Bill had been made to carry out 120 hours of community service for assaulting Mr Johnson. I hadn't attended court. I felt I should have been there, supporting him, but I couldn't; I couldn't risk Rosie and me being exposed to the press. If Bill was hurt when I went to see him, he hid it well.

I looked up at the sky. It was closing in fast on me. I was half tempted to just head straight home, which was the sensible thing to do. But then I was so close to the river, I just had to run down to see her silvery waters flowing fast down into the town. I was there within seconds and I sat on the bank gazing into the river as the sun melted into her and she turned from gold to black.

I was so engrossed I didn't notice footsteps behind me.

'Here, talking to yourself again, Ms Myrtle? What will the townfolk say?'

I turned with a start. It was the vicar. Here we were

again, back in the place where it had all started. He seemed more weasel-like every day. I knew he was just a hatchet man, carrying out the unpleasant assignments given to him by the mayor. It didn't suit him to act the way he was doing.

'Hello, Vicar,' I said, composing myself. 'How's Mr Johnson?'

'Better, but no thanks to you. You do realise if he'd have passed, God bless his soul, that you would have blood on your hands?'

'I don't know what you're talking about, Vicar, I wasn't even there.' I was getting tired of this accusation. Even though no one in the town had said this to me directly before, it was written all over their faces.

The vicar leaned heavily on his Malacca cane; he was showing signs of ageing. I felt sorry for him at that moment. How had the poor man been so foolish as to get involved in such blackmail? I decided to appeal to his lighter, more devout side.

'How's your wife, Vicar? I'd heard she was feeling a little under the weather. I've made some cherry cakes and was thinking of dropping one into her for you both to share.'

This caught him off guard. He looked confused and wearier than before. In some ways he reminded me of my father. I felt saddened that, had we met in kinder circumstances, we may have been friends.

He composed himself, taking on the devilish composure of the mayor once more.

'I've heard how you talk to the animals in the forest,' he said. 'I've been watching you, every time you step foot out of that rundown shack of a house you call home, I'm there watching you. You should have watched your step, Vivian. You should have heeded the advice I told Dennis to give you: to lock yourself away up there and not come out.'

Dennis had said that but Barbara, as usual, had just pooh-poohed everything he said. But surely that was for my own good, wasn't it? Was he just twisting what he'd seen to suit his own vindictive means or had he actually asked Dennis to tell me that? Dennis was a churchgoer but then I'd always thought he was on my side. Who would have thought this awful racket could have brought us so low as to have sides?

'Yes, Ms Myrtle, I've been watching you. And at the request of the congregation, I shall be reporting back to them. I'm afraid you leave me no choice. I've tried to be patient. I shall have to tell them if you're not a witch then you're clinically insane.'

Insane. The words struck an awful chord with me, whisking me straight out of the forest, away from the safety of Cherrystone Cottage back to my dangerous, vicious husband. I felt dizzy, my head began to spin.

'You know I'm right don't you, Vivian?' cackled the vicar, noting my reaction.

I tried to steady myself. But all I could see was abuse, arguments, tantrums, sadness, and patronising doctors in white coats.

'They'll take you away, you do realise that?' said the vicar. 'They'll take you away from here.'

By now his voice was distant, echoing and rattling around in my ears: they'll take you away, away from Cherrystone Cottage, away from Ivory Meadows, from the campaign, from Bill, Barbara, Miss Metford ... from Rosie?

The vicar continued, his voice now quieter, kinder, less like he was enjoying himself, 'It'll be for your own good, my dear. It'll make you feel better. You've been under a lot of pressure recently. It'll calm your over-heightened senses, steady your nerves.'

I could see his lips moving but they didn't correspond with the words that seemed to be floating around me in the night air. I could see them spelt out, illuminated like the glow-worms in the glade: 'feel better', 'steady', 'witch', 'senses', 'nerves', 'own good'.

I could see them but they didn't make any sense, they jumbled in my mind as I desperately tried to work out what they meant. My own thoughts became illuminated next to the words in the air: 'take away Rosie', 'leave Cherrystone Cottage'.

'Of course, if you were to just leave of your own accord, the town could go back to normal and everyone would be happy once again. It doesn't do to yearn for things that are simply out of one's reach. Far better to be satisfied with one's lot.'

Satisfied with our lot. Those were the words of my ex-husband, Jack. A picture of him flashed up in my mind. I began to feel sick. I could feel my whole body starting to tremble just at the thought of him.

'I shall advise the congregation we'll be asking the doctor to come round to do some tests. It will make you feel good about yourself again, Vivian. I have been so worried about you.'

Worried about you, those were Jack's words too, when he was having a nice moment. Rosie, Jack, the cottage, our journey to Ivory Meadows, Miss Metford, Bill, everything flashed before me. It was like I saw my whole life in black-and-white pictures within the space of a couple of seconds.

'Are you all right, Vivian? I didn't mean to upset you.'

I felt myself starting to fall. It felt like a relief to start with, my weight, the weight of the world, being taken from me. Then I realised I couldn't steady myself. The vicar lunged forward to grab me but I backed off. I fell and fell, everything spinning before me like a whirlpool of my life.

'Vivian, no …' he screamed.

The water cracked like an enormous sheet of glass when I hit it. I went under, grateful to the murky depths for catching and cradling me in her arms. I sank lower and lower, passing fish, weeds, broken bottles and bits of rusty cars. Here everything was calm and tranquil, dark and motherly. The voices had gone.

Then I tried to breathe.

I gulped and gasped in horror, taking in mouthfuls of dirty, polluted water. I tried to scramble my way up to the top but a reed had caught my ankle and was pulling me down further. I could see a light shining brightly at what I assumed was the top of the river but it felt like it was a hundred miles away.

I struggled and managed to free my leg. Now I was moving, twisting and turning in the fast-paced river.

I swam desperately towards the light, trying to stop the panic from making me swallow too much water. I reached the top and broke free with an almighty crash, smashing the smooth surface of the water with my head and gasping desperately for air. The water was moving fast and was as cold as ice. I looked over to the bank. The vicar was waving and holding out a branch for me to grab hold of. He was screaming that he was sorry and he had only been saying those things to try to get me to leave for my own good; that he didn't mean it and was only carrying out Mr Johnson's wishes from his hospital bed. But he was too far away. I tried to swim back, against the current, to reach the branch. I was a strong swimmer but my dress, coat and shoes weighed me down. I glanced again at the bank. The vicar had gone. I prayed it was to get help. Surely a man of the cloth couldn't be so wicked as to abandon me to drown.

Drown. As the word came into my mind I realised that was exactly what I was doing. I panicked and went under again. The still calmness of the murky underwater felt easy and comforting. But I couldn't give up; I had to get back to Rosie.

I tugged at the buttons on my coat and tried to rip it off

my back. It clung to me like a dead weight. I battled with it and eventually it came free and floated to the surface. I gulped another mouthful of air and then kicked off my shoes. Less weighted down, I found I was able to keep my head above water. I swam, desperately searching for something to grab hold of, something to take me back to the safety of the riverside. Back to the sanctuary of my home and daughter.

By now, it was pitch black and virtually impossible to see. I was shivering violently in the inky black water. Suddenly I saw lights ahead. The town. I felt a surge of energy soar through my blood, turning it into fire. My body grew hotter and I felt strength in my bones. I would survive. I lifted my right arm and pushed it through the water. I did the same with my left. It took such great effort. As I neared the town, helped by the current, the light illuminated a branch overhanging the river.

Right arm, left arm, right arm, left arm.

I started powering towards the branch. I couldn't let the river take me past it. It was my only hope. Mustering all my strength, I leapt out of the water and grabbed the branch but it was wet and slimy and my hands slid straight off it. I turned to grab it again but it was too late. The river had already swept me beyond it.

This is it, I thought, I'm going to die here in this watery grave. I was too exhausted to save myself, even for Rosemary's sake. Maybe the vicar was right, maybe she and the people here were better off without me. I started taking in more water. Big gulps of mucky brown liquid. It tasted foul but perhaps this was the last supper I deserved. I'd clearly not been a good enough wife, I was a lousy mother, and I'd brought disrepute, brawling, fire, and scandal to a tiny town where nothing normally happened. My just desserts were that my body would be bloated with disgusting soapy scum and there was nothing I could do about it.

Suddenly, I bumped into the riverbank. There was a section that jutted out more than the rest and it had 'caught' me. I didn't know whether to laugh or cry. Instinctively I clung to it but in my heart of hearts I wasn't sure whether I'd already decided my fate. What had I to live for? Rosie would have a better life with a better mother.

Then I heard a scream, followed by lots of shouting. Two sets of arms hauled me up off the bank and onto the riverside. There I lay lifeless, motionless. My body was so tired I could have just let it go there and then, could have drifted off into a better world where I could be a better person. I could hear a siren and thought I saw a flashing light although I'm sure my eyes were closed. There was lots of talking and general commotion and then I felt hands on my body.

The next thing I knew I was lying in a hospital bed. I jumped up, panicking. Had I been committed as the vicar had suggested?

'Hello, Vivian, love, we thought we'd lost you for a moment last night,' said Barbara. She was stood at the end of the bed. Rosie rushed over and threw her arms around me.

Last night? What happened last night?

'Don't quite know how you managed it but you ended up in the river. It was lucky Bill spotted you and called to Dennis. The pair of them hauled you out. Just at that moment the vicar came down the road, screaming that you were dead. He'd found your clothes further upstream in the river. He was beside himself; I've never seen a man so upset. Don't talk now, dear. You can tell me everything when you're feeling more like yourself again.'

More myself? Who was that? It all came back to me. Last night I'd wanted to kill that person.

Barbara said she'd give me a minute and would be

outside should I want anything. After she'd gone, Rosie buried her head in my neck and sobbed.

'I thought you were going to die, Mummy. First you didn't come home and I got worried, so did Barbara. Then Bill came running in saying you'd been taken to hospital. He was soaking wet.'

'Don't worry, darling,' I said, stroking her golden hair. 'I'm here now and I'm never going to leave you again.'

I knew I meant it. All those thoughts yesterday were just the demented curses the vicar had put into my head. He'd done much more than cause an accident, he had made me allow myself to be frightened. Really frightened.

After many checks by the nurses and doctors, and some questioning, I was allowed back home. Dennis drove us there, sat quietly in the front with Barbara, while Rosie and I held hands in the back. It was a relief to get back into the haven of our cottage.

Barbara stayed with me for two days until I was back on my feet again. On the morning of the third day, she popped back to the shop to pick up some groceries for me. When she came back her face was ashen.

'What's wrong?' I asked.

'The rumours in the town have become worse. It's been said you must be a witch – simply due to the fact you survived and didn't drown.'

'Oh my God,' I said, clutching my hands to my face. 'Would people really believe such nonsense? It's such an old myth.'

'Oh, you remember the story?' nodded Barbara. 'It was one of the things Maureen and Mrs Donaldson discovered when they were helping Janice with her research for ghost hunts. They used to do it here, centuries ago. Susan Merrick, a local woman, was drowned that way, according to the books in the library, so Janice was telling me. She stood trial and was taken to the river. Everyone in the town came to watch, so says the legend. If

92

she survived, she was a witch and would be hanged. If she drowned then she wasn't a witch after all and really that was just her bad luck. Unbelievable, really, but there you go. You witches have always had a hard time,' she chuckled.

'Lock yourself away and don't come out. You should have heeded the advice I told Dennis to tell you.' The vicar's words came flooding back to me. Did Barbara and Dennis really believe I was a witch? Had she been sent to supposedly look after me as a cover up for being a spy for the clergy?

'I'm joking, of course, Vivian,' she said gently. I must have given away my thoughts. It seemed I could trust nobody, not even my own thoughts.

'So what happened to Susan Merrick?' I asked, trying to divert the subject away from myself.

'She drowned. No one was taught to swim then unless they were the sons of the fishermen. Though some say when she was washed up there were stones in her pockets.'

'Cursed, small-minded community!' I exclaimed, suddenly not caring if I came across as bitter and twisted. 'Why on earth do they keep on with such stupidity? Although I suppose I should be grateful. I think I'd rather be burnt on a stake than sent to an asylum.'

'What are you talking about, love?'

She seemed genuinely surprised. Perhaps the vicar hadn't mentioned his 'observations' after all.

'You're still confused, Vivian, you've been through a wretched ordeal. Don't worry, Dennis and I will see that no harm comes to you.'

'I suppose it would have been quite convenient had I died. I'd have just been out of his hair and, as he said, everything could go back to how it was before I arrived.'

'Who are you talking about, love?'

'No one,' I mumbled. I didn't want to add further fuel to the fire.

Barbara kissed me affectionately on the cheek and returned to run her shop, which she said had been a shambles since she'd left Dennis in charge. Was she Judas? She and Dennis had shown me nothing but kindness. Could they betray me so badly?

That night I dreamt of a sparse, weed-infested garden. Perhaps it was as a result of seeing those twisted reeds of the river and feeling them pulling me down. I awoke unnerved and turned on the light to find a dream analogy guide I'd borrowed from the library. My dream seemed to suggest I was neglecting my spiritual needs. What could they be? I felt I was fully in tune with my feelings, perhaps a little too so at times. I hoped it didn't mean I needed to start attending church; I doubted I'd be allowed through the doors.

I settled back to sleep and, when I awoke the next day, I was surprised to find I'd slept through until late morning. I knew my near-death experience had exhausted me but I was shocked Rosemary had allowed me to stay in bed so long. Pulling on my dressing gown, I went into her room. It was quiet and the curtains were still drawn. My little girl looked up at me with big trembling eyes.

'What is it, sweetheart?' I asked, smoothing her fringe away from her forehead. I realised her face and hair was soaking wet. My poor baby was feverish.

'I can't move, Mummy,' she whimpered.

'You poor thing. Let Mummy get you a wet face cloth to cool you down.'

'I'm tied to the bed,' said Rosemary, 'the fairies have fastened my arms and legs to the bedposts.'

I looked under the covers and picked up her arms and legs. They fell lifelessly back to the bed like dead weights. Not only was she weak, but she was delirious, too.

I made her comfortable then went into the kitchen to brew a broth of healing herbs and spices to make her well.

While I was stirring all the love I had for her into the pot, I realised it had been a long time since I had stopped to take this time out of my busy schedule for her.

Was I to blame for this illness by leaving her alone playing with her beloved fairies for far too long? Had she picked up on the awful rumours the mayor had been spreading about us around the town? Was she scared her mother was a witch?

Suddenly it dawned on me. My dream had nothing to do with my selfish needs, it was Rosemary's spiritual needs I'd been neglecting. Had I been a good mother, I would have been there to answer all her questions rather than being stood here now wondering what was going through her precious seven-year-old head. She had been through an awful lot in the past year.

I went back up to her bedroom, fed her medicine and soothing soup, mopped her furrowed brow, and tied a red ribbon in her hair to try to prevent the illness from worsening. I cuddled and nursed her. How could I have so neglected the only thing that was ever really important to me? How had we gone so far?

Chapter Eight

My mother's healing potions did nothing for Rosie. She still seemed delirious, calling out names and talking of babies. I knew we had to visit the doctor. As I walked through the streets of Ivory Meadows I saw women ushering their children to the other side of the road, trying to protect them from even setting eyes on me. Some busy-bodies stopped and stared, others looked away, pretending not to have noticed me at all.

One woman, whose name I didn't know, spat out a venomous barrage of words at me. I was tired, my little girl was desperately ill. I just turned and walked away.

Dr Miller was sympathetic, thankfully. He said Rosie had a nasty virus and prescribed antibiotics, telling me she needed plenty of rest until she was fully recovered. However, Mrs Whitley, the chemist's wife, was reluctant to serve me to start with until I cast her an evil glare. I knew it would do nothing to help my cause but that didn't matter right now, all that mattered was my little girl.

I stayed by Rosemary's side day and night, stroking her head gently as she slept.

'*Fais de beaux rêves*, my angel,' I whispered, hoping her dreams might be better than the nightmare I seemed to keep putting her through.

On the third day, she vastly improved, so we spent all morning in the garden, playing, dancing, and laughing. It felt just like it did when we had first arrived at Cherrystone

Cottage. Coming in out of the cold, we settled down to a feast of hot, buttered crumpets and steaming mugs of hot chocolate, topped with cream and marshmallows, just the way Rosie liked it. In the afternoon, we sat in front of the fire, telling each other stories. I helped her with her homework, geed on by the promise of black cherry tart and custard for tea. It was a Mummy and Rosemary day, and it was very long overdue.

I must say it did rather feel like the calm after a storm. I couldn't believe just how much had gone on in such a short space of time. Rosie seemed much improved thanks to our lovely day together but she still remained far happier playing with Whisper in her room than spending time with her mum. She painted huge, wild, fanciful paintings, usually of fairies. In one they were dancing around the garden, in another they were kneeling in a circle round a wise old wizard, another showed them building fairy homes out of twigs and leaves. There was one that stood apart from all the others. It was all black apart from a series of beautiful stars in silver and gold. They seemed to shimmer off the page. It was a charming picture, simple yet darkly menacing and strangely mesmerising at the same time. When I asked her about it, she said: 'Don't you recognise it, Mummy? It's our garden, the garden of stars.'

The garden of stars. I suppose that's exactly what it was. A garden of dreams but more than that, it was a place where you absolutely believed they could come true. I adored my daughter, her spirit was breathtaking. I wondered whether my dreams would come true.

Rosie loved school and was itching to get back there. I, too, decided it was time to face the music once and for all. I put on my favourite black dress, my pink shawl, and my pink high heels – the clothes I'd first arrived in. I wanted to feel good and confident and I knew this outfit was the best for the job. I put on plenty of make-up, dropped off Rosie, explaining to her teacher that she needed to take it easy, then carried on into the town.

I decided to pay Gillian a visit first. I knew she would be hard to win over so I thought I'd tackle her before she could pick up on any tittle-tattle from others that the 'witch on the hill' had dared show her face in town.

She had her back turned to me as I approached. The bell on her shop door tinkled as I walked in, closing the door and cold air out behind me. She turned and dropped all the red roses she was arranging onto the floor.

'What are you doing here?' she asked, backing away into the corner.

The red flowers and their prickly thorns looked like a river of blood and rage between us.

'I didn't mean to make you jump,' I said, gently. I had expected anger, abuse, fireworks even, but not fear.

'I don't know exactly what's been said about me but I can imagine,' I said. 'I plotted to burn down Mr Shaw's house, put the mayor in hospital and Bill in jail. Oh, and I suppose the fact I didn't drown recently only goes to prove I'm a witch.'

She cowered as I said the word. It echoed and rattled round the walls of the shop. 'Something like that,' she mumbled.

'I have just one question for you, Gillian,' I said, being careful not to move or edge closer. Heaven knows she might think I was casting a spell on her. 'And that is, had I been an evil witch why would I have worked so tirelessly to save Mr Shaw and everyone else's homes from demolition, to try to prevent Bill's shop from closing down, and to enable this to be a fantastic place to live?'

Gillian started to come forward. 'I knew you'd say that but you're just trying to twist my thoughts, make me think you're a decent person. Well, it won't work with me, Vivian Myrtle, and it won't work with the rest of the town either.'

'How exactly have I hurt you, Gillian?'

'By being a selfish, strange woman who thought she'd use a town's hardship as a means of making friends!' By now she was shouting and stood right in front of me, refusing to show her fear anymore.

'Maybe you're right.' I sighed, plonking myself down amongst the mass of red petals. 'I just loved this town the minute I stepped foot in it – the little train that brought us here, the wonderful open hills, the cool, dark forests, the extraordinary wildlife, and the extraordinary people, too. I felt a bond with people here that I hadn't felt in a long, long time.'

'So if you felt all that, if we believe it, then why did you betray us so badly?'

'How did I betray you, Gillian?'

'By not telling us the truth.'

There it was. The truth, that horribly suffocating noose around my neck.

'I know I'm a bit of an enigma, and that you don't understand why I turned up here out of the blue and why I'm not married. I'm separated if you must know ... on the run from my abusive husband, if that helps.'

Gillian slowly came over and slumped down next to my side. Gently, she took my hand in hers. 'I'm sorry, Vivian, I didn't know.'

'It's not your fault, how could you? I didn't want to burden other people with it; it was my own cross to bear. And throwing myself into the campaign helped to take my mind off it a little. I suppose you could say I used it to make me feel better. But you have to understand that was only because I felt for the first time I was doing something good, not something to make money, or to climb the career ladder or to improve my status but something honest and wholesome and good. I've not been able to save the good things in my life; I wanted to save something good here.

And that landed me as a witch.'

She paused, staring at me. 'I was almost tarnished with the same brush myself when Miles left,' she said, slowly. 'He was my other half. It was quite a scandal when I fell pregnant with Patricia because we'd not been together long. Thing was we never really wanted to stay together, it was just an accident, a very good accident, but an accident nonetheless. We tried it out for a couple of years, being a couple that is, but it just wasn't working so we both decided it was for the best that he left.

'That was seventeen years ago now. I think some of the locals are still only just coming to terms with it.' She sniggered. 'Best thing that happened to me, though. I prefer to be a free spirit. You'll see, you and Rosie will be better off, too.'

I nodded, keeping my eyes on the floor. I didn't know what to say. I was grateful to her for sharing her story with me but I was still too scared of my past creeping up on me to reveal the extent of mine.

'Suppose you'd better help me pick up these roses then,' she said, nudging me as she knelt forward to grab one stem at a time.

I joined her instantly. She wasn't one to show emotion. This was Gillian's way of telling me she understood, she didn't need any more information, and she certainly didn't want any tears messing up her flower shop floor.

As I stepped out of her shop, the air felt crisp and fresh. I felt more confident in taking on the rest of the town. Gillian had shown me it was reassurance they wanted not arguments. I hadn't, however, counted on using the sympathy vote and I didn't intend to use it again.

Bill seemed pleased to see me when I wandered into his shop. He looked tired from all the extra hours he was having to put in at the community centre.

'I'm sorry, Bill,' I said, 'I never meant to get you into so much trouble, I don't even know if I should be here

101

now but I had to see you.'

'Don't be daft, Viv, glad you came. You weren't there that night, someone had to pantomime stand up for you. Looks like it pantomime-well had to be me.'

I smiled. 'I'm grateful to you. Bill, do you still feel like that now after everything that's been said since?'

'Listen, love, I was the one what pulled you out of those waters, you looked pretty drowned to me.'

'So you do think I'm a witch?'

He fidgeted uncomfortably. 'Well, what about all those messages in code, those special teas and those herbs in your garden? I'm not a particularly religious man, Vivian, don't really bother me either way, just want to know, that's all.'

I coughed to smother a laugh. He was a loveable oaf at times.

'The codes were common sense under the circumstances,' I explained. 'Barbara told you that at the time. The tea and cakes are just my form of hospitality. And the herbs are just old wives' tales my mother used to tell me. Don't you carry on things your folks passed onto you, no matter how silly they seem?'

He paused, then nodded. 'Don't suppose you've got any of that cherry cake going spare have you, Viv?' he laughed, cheekily.

'Of course, why don't you pop round later?'

I was doing well. And yet, the Donaldsons and Maureen Sprockett, the librarian, weren't so easily won over. They ranted myths and legends at me like I was some kind of leper. They had clearly spent too much time with their heads buried in fanciful stories of the past, and to think that careful study had been my suggestion too. I'd never heard anything so ridiculous but that was the power of the gossip machine. It was taken as gospel, especially considering who turned the wheel.

As they stomped off into the distance, I cried, 'How

could I be a witch when I gave you all a pot of rosemary as a symbol of our friendship? Don't you know that rosemary planted by the doorstep keeps witches away?'

Barbara told it straight. 'Basically,' she said, 'the people here like you. Try as they might, they can't see it in their hearts to wish someone misfortune who they've spent so many happy hours with. It's probably a good thing you've come down now. They just needed to see for themselves you hadn't grown a long green nose and warts.' She chuckled.

'But Barbara, I have a question for you. Why did you do as the vicar asked by telling me to hide away?'

'Love, you've misunderstood that man from the start. He does have everyone's best interests at heart really, yours included. He's just got himself into a bit of stupid pickle with the mayor. Whatever he said to you down at the river, I'm sure it was meant with the best intentions; probably, knowing him, to save you from a great fall in pride. Unfortunately you went and had another fall instead.

'Believe it or not, he actually wanted your campaign to win. That's why he volunteered to come to the classes instead of the mayor, he just reported mumbo-jumbo back and Mr Johnson was none the wiser. That's also probably why he volunteered the information to you about him being blackmailed in the first place. But now, everyone knows it's just too late. Everything stopped the moment Bill got into trouble. There's been chaos ever since, which is why we've done nothing with the posters either. I'm afraid we can't do anything now, love, we may as well give in gracefully and still have somewhere to live rather than making ourselves homeless in the process.'

Walking back up the hill, I felt numb. It turned out that when the planners and architects had visited with their clipboards, the townspeople had just buried their heads in the sand and tried to pretend it wasn't happening. The mayor's brother had come in with the offer of having brand new houses for them all; no wonder they were prepared to shut up and put up. How convenient that I'd been out of sight and out of mind. I was just told I didn't have as much at stake as everyone else as Cherrystone Cottage was rented, not bought. The thought of my beautiful cottage with her buttermilk walls, English country garden, dark corners, and sooty hearths being bulldozed without me having any say in the matter was just too much. It broke my heart in two. I thought of all the fun Rosie and I had enjoyed there. It was too much a part of our lives to break away from it; it was like there were three of us in our relationship: me, Rosie, and the house.

Then there were the woods and hills around us. All those wonderful walks: dawn, noon, and dusk. The birds, the centuries-old trees, the fish, the deer, the pheasants, the otters. They would all be obliterated. The latest plans I'd read were for a further 3,000 homes to be built on two hundred hectares of forest and fields.

That night I dreamt of a phoenix rising up from the ashes. I awoke in the middle of the night with a start. That was it! The secret lay in Mr Shaw's house. Perhaps the scorched remains of his home could hold the key to unlocking the secret of Ivory Meadows.

I jumped out of bed and, checking Rosie was still fast asleep, threw my raincoat on over my night dress, pulled on my boots and hat, and ran out into the darkness. It was drizzling as I grabbed the spade from out of the shed and began to walk down the hill. I knew I'd only just redeemed my sanity in the eyes of the community and that this would look highly suspicious but I was driven to do it.

As I approached the town the rain became much heavier, it felt like it was pounding on my back. I'd come too far now to turn back. I reached Mr Shaw's house and, glancing around me to check no one was watching, I ducked under the police cordon signs and tiptoed into what was left of the scorched property. The roof was half missing, which was in some ways a blessing as it meant that although I got wet, I could see what I was doing by the light of the moon. It was a creepy, harrowing, lonely place. An overturned, singed chair sat next to a blown-out television. The remains of what looked like a photograph album were scattered on the floor, the pictures presumably the ashes I was wading through. A door was lying flat on the ground, hooks on the back of it still holding Jake's leads. It sent a chill down my spine. I wished I'd put on some warmer clothing.

I scanned the room, searching for something, anything of any value to my desperate, abandoned campaign.

The floorboards were up, exposing raw muddy ground underneath what had once been a comfortable living room.

I started to dig, carefully at first, not wanting to disturb the solemn gloom of the place too much, then frantically. I felt something must lie under those floorboards, under this hallowed ground. I was there for around an hour but I found nothing. I collapsed, exhausted, next to the big hole I'd created. Perhaps I was going mad after all. Dispirited, I began to return all the earth to its rightful place. Once everything looked as dismal as it had when I arrived, I made my way out of the house and up the path until something nearly tripped me over. I looked down to see a bone. It must have been one of Jake's he'd buried in the garden. That was the secret. I'd been searching and it was right in front of me all the time. Clutching it in my pocket I ran back up the hill, making it through the front door just as the birds were starting to salute sun up.

All day in the shop, I tried to keep myself occupied so I didn't give anything away to Barbara. I remained unsure as to whether she was a sneak but, either way, I knew what I was about to do was going to cause trouble and I didn't want anyone else responsible for it. Even Rosie had commented on how happy and smiley I'd been that morning but I hadn't let on about my secret.

That night, after I'd tucked Rosie into bed, reading her favourite *Melissa the Amazing Pink Princess* story to her first and later checking she was fast asleep, I once again threw my coat, scarf, and gloves on and ventured into my own back garden. The skeleton I'd tried to bury and forget was going to be resurrected. Luckily I knew exactly where she was hidden; it was hard not to. It took me a good hour to remove the tiny bones from the shallow grave. I tried not to think too much about what I was doing. I knew it was wrong to tamper with bones that had been laid to rest, but I felt they had been calling out to us from the start. This baby's life was not over yet, she could not rest until her existence, however short, had been worthwhile. I liked to think I was helping her to heaven, to a place where she could finally rest peacefully. I carefully placed the miniature skeleton into a huge bag and, heaving it over my shoulder, I walked like Robin Hood, into the town in the darkness once more, back to Mr Shaw's house. It was clear nobody had visited since the night before and my freshly dug earth was easy enough to lift once more. I buried the bones as deeply as I could then packed down the earth to make it look untouched.

Wearily, I climbed the hill and eventually the stairs back up to my bed. I was exhausted.

Early the next morning, before work, I sent two anonymous letters. One was to a historian's guild saying old documents had been found, which showed evidence of a plague that had hit the area hundreds of years before. Maureen had shown me research on this, but we had ruled it out as irrelevant to our campaign, apart from perhaps a display in the library, but now I saw its significance. Nothing would be wasted in our endeavour to save our town; there were too few of us for that. The second letter was to the local newspaper office, claiming that I had

106

spotted a man acting suspiciously around Mr Shaw's house who, when questioned, said he was a keen archaeologist who believed the house had been built over a series of unmarked graves possibly relevant to his ancestors. Could one of their reporters, I asked the editor, make some enquiries at the local historian's guild to find out whether there was any truth in these claims? With each letter, I drew a map to show the spot. I even stained the map to the historian's guild with coffee and singed it round the edges for added authenticity. Now all I had to do was wait.

Sure enough, a local reporter arrived in no time, along with a member of the local historian's guild. They began asking lots of questions. I knew I was taking a risk with what I was doing but I could see no other option. I kept my head down and didn't get involved. There was no way I wanted my face in the newspaper. I think Maureen quite liked being the centre of attention, proudly showing them the display boards she'd been working on for the library. At work, Barbara said Maureen had told her the man from the historian's guild was seeking permission from Mr Shaw and the police to begin digging. I was suddenly struck with guilt that I would be unintentionally causing extra upset to the poor old man. When I asked Barbara how he was coping, she said he was just as intrigued as the rest of us and had happily given them the green light to go ahead. Good old Mr Shaw. I could have rushed round and hugged him, would it not have blown my cover. I quickly changed the subject with Barbara, quietly smiling to myself as I went to make us both a cup of tea.

It seemed to take forever for the police to give their blessing to the dig, although really it was only a matter of days. But when the historian's guild discovered the tiny skeleton, it was as if the circus had come to town.

Suddenly the focus had changed. The national press was tantalised by a sniff of intrigue and it hit the headlines. Ivory Meadows was back in the papers again, and although the reporters made reference to the previous incidents to remind their readers where this tiny town was based, those events were old news now and seemed insignificant. *The Times* did an entire feature on the value of retaining history in small towns, with Ivory Meadows as the main town, with pictures of the church, the bridge, Bill, Barbara, and the vicar.

It was a glorious article and everyone was delighted.

And, within no time, we received a piece of news that was better than we could have dreamed of: a top historian had taken great interest in the article in *The Times*, done his own investigations, and found further historical interest, which was, of course, a great relief to me. He held a meeting with the town council and there it was declared that parts of Ivory Meadows were of national historical interest and therefore nothing could be touched there until further research was carried out and the appropriate listings made. We rejoiced that no building work could commence. I knew at some point I would have to come clean about the skeleton in my garden but that was something I would worry about at a later stage. All that mattered now was that we'd temporarily halted the ticking time bomb over our town.

We decided to celebrate and for once Rosie and I actually joined everyone in The Mason Arms for a drink. It was nice to be welcomed again. Bill made a slightly drunken speech about how pleased he was, both for the town and that he had been let off the hook with just community service. He went onto say he'd do it all again until Ian, the landlord, abruptly quietened him down.

Once everyone was chatting away in their little groups again, I made my way over to Barbara, Dennis, and Bill, who were sitting at a small, round table together.

'Come on over, love,' said Barbara, eagerly.

I grabbed my opportunity, took a deep breath and whispered that, in light of what had happened, perhaps we ought to use the lovely posters we had created to revive the campaign again. There was just over a week to go until the start of advent.

Bill whistled between his lips; Dennis scowled. I thought I'd gone too far again. Then Barbara tutted at the two men next to her.

'Don't pay them any attention, Vivian, love.' She smiled. 'We were just saying the exact same thing but we were concerned you might not want to have anything to do with it, what with everything that's gone on. And the way everyone has acted, too,' she sighed, glumly.

'Not at all.' I laughed. 'Leave it with me.'

Chapter Nine

Everyone was cheerful and happy on the way into work the following morning, each smugly bidding each other good day, knowing we were soon to release our campaign to try to put the final seal on Ivory Meadows' salvation. We'd heard that Mr Johnson had made a full recovery and was back in town again. I, for one, was glad he was well but not especially looking forward to seeing him.

Barbara was particularly chirpy. By all accounts she'd celebrated with a few too many sherries in the pub the night before and Dennis had had to carry her home and put her to bed. Although her head was a little sore, she looked youthful and mischievous; she was doing things she'd not done in years.

Each customer who came into the shop was full of news. They had plans of how they proposed to refurbish their homes, discussions as to whether we should see about bringing a cinema back to Ivory Meadows, whether it would be possible to continue yoga classes in, perhaps, a more exercise-based manner. There was a buzz about the place I had never witnessed before.

Even Dennis was pleased. He said the town's new-found vigour was obviously making people hungry as we'd sold far more than usual. I heard Barbara singing softly to herself, and I even caught a glimpse of the couple stealing a kiss in the storeroom.

Suddenly a huge gong was heard in the town. It rang again, this time quieter and more muffled than before. The eerie sound it gave off stopped everyone in their tracks. It was an awful toll, like a doomsday signal.

It took a few, long painful seconds for the dreadful reality of what was happening to sink in. I'd been so engrossed with trying to fit all the potatoes into one basket on the shelf, I hadn't realised straight away there's only one set of bells in the town. The church! I screamed out to Barbara and we ran together out onto the street. We had to get there before the vicar, pretty impossible really when we realised he was inside, having his usual Friday meeting with potential wedding couples. This couple had obviously asked about the wedding bells.

The bells had never been used in all the time I'd been there – apart from the vicar's return from honeymoon, which had signalled their end as it had seemed he didn't want to hear them again after his so-called welcome-home party.

Turning the corner, I could see the mighty church that stood, foreboding, in the middle of the town. In the dim autumn light, it seemed to loom larger than life. It was no wonder the people of Ivory Meadows were so guided by everything the vicar told them, their place of worship threatened them every time they came into town. I shuddered just looking at the doorway. It brought back memories, feelings I'd banished to the very depths of my soul.

The bells continued to ring, muffled and hollow, seeming to turn everything into slow motion. I ran there as fast as I could with Barbara in tow. Bill brought up the rear as he had guessed what was about to happen too: if the bells were muffled something was hidden in the bell tower. It didn't take much to work that out. The mayor arrived just as we did. He and Bill eyed each other up suspiciously, like two terriers about to be let off their leashes. We were at stalemate, neither party wanting to move to give away the game. Mr Johnson looked just as he always had done, if anything he looked healthier and refreshed. I wondered if he'd eked out his time in hospital just to make matters worse for Bill.

Then the vicar came walking out of the church with great armfuls of our leaflets and posters. As he lifted one to read it, I tried to snatch it out of his hand, and in doing so I forced him to drop the lot. Just then an almighty gust of wind lifted the pile off the street and into the air. Suddenly there were papers everywhere, like a huge kaleidoscope of colour, swishing and swirling gracefully in front of our faces. First, we were all too stunned to move then, coming to our senses, we tried desperately to grab them. But it was too late, the wind had already taken possession of them and was carrying them away. The mayor managed to grab a leaflet and took great delight in reading out its contents.

'Come to Ivory Meadows,' he scoffed, 'to get ready for Christmas the good old-fashioned way. We have steam train rides, Santa special riverboat cruises, arts and crafts, gift-making workshops for children in the museum, gastro festive cookery classes for adults. This pretty Georgian town is a must-see, come join the fun.'

There was even a little map on the bottom to show people exactly where we were on the River Forsayth.

Mr Johnson cackled with delight: 'What a shame these leaflets won't reach any of the people they were intended for. Never mind, it's probably saved everyone a lot of time and effort because none of this will be here by the time you'd have got these out.'

The vicar butted in, 'I do actually think it's a tremendous shame really, Mayor. I think these leaflets are rather nice, don't you?'

'Shut up, you bumbling fool.'

This clearly enraged Mr Baker. His face turned quite red. 'You've felt that way about me for too long now,' he stuttered. 'This whole situation has gone too far.

113

'Someone almost died as a result of your scheming,' he added, glancing nervously over at me. 'I may have my faults but a man of the cloth never causes human suffering or loss of life. I'm truly sorry, Vivian, I feel wholly responsible for what happened to you.'

He bent his head in shame.

I could hardly believe my ears, and I didn't know what to say.

'You had nothing to do with what happened to Vivian, Vicar,' ranted Mr Johnson. 'It was all her own doing. Had I been here things would never have got to this stage in any case.'

The vicar's head shot up again. He caught the mayor's gaze and fixed it with his own eyes. His red, flustered face had disappeared. He looked strong and resolute.

'You being away in hospital gave me time to think,' he said. 'Ivory Meadows was a much nicer place without you here, and I think if you were to leave, it would be for the best. You scared me with your blackmail, Mr Johnson, but people know about the enormous financial debt I owe you and that I shall pay it back, too. I have talked it through with my wife and she understands. There's no need for me to be blackmailed over it anymore.'

Barbara clasped her hands together in joy then ran over to hug him. We were all thrilled that he, of all people, had at last seen the light.

Mr Johnson piped up: 'Yes, yes, that's all very nice. Have a little kiss and cuddle, pay off your debts and make up. You don't think it'll be that simple, do you? I didn't come here to make friends. I came here to make money. And for the amount of time and personal injury I've endured here,' he glared at Bill, 'I'm certainly going to get everything I deserve.

'You didn't think a few old bones would save the town, did you?' he cackled to everyone, relishing the attention and ignoring Bill as he made to step forward but was stopped by Dennis.

'A couple of decrepit historians are hardly going to stand in my way. My family has money, you know, and money equals power. As we speak, the planning officers at the council are already setting dates to overrule the temporary halt in work so that we can get started on what will actually, for once, be of benefit to the people of Ivory Meadows. I have, of course, always had your interests at heart. I bid you all, and your little leaflets, good day.'

With that he strolled off pompously, over the bridge and out of town.

My mind was racing, everyone was asking what should be done, even the vicar, which seemed strangely out of character. I was pleased he'd changed his mind, I'd always felt in my heart he was a good man.

'Leave it with me,' I said. 'Collect Rosie from school and give her some tea for me, would you please, Barbara? I don't know now whether our tourism campaign will make any difference but it's all we've got so I'll see to it personally that the carnival still goes ahead a week tomorrow.'

Clutching what remained of the posters and leaflets, I ran up the hill back home as fast as my legs would carry me.

Chapter Ten

Mary Metford arrived while I was running around in a frenzy.

'What on earth is the matter with you, girl; have you gone crazy?'

'Not yet, Miss Metford, although I think I must be nearing it. I'm trying to write a press release and I've got to get these original leaflets and posters to the printers in the city. It will close in two hours and we can't afford to waste a whole weekend. I can't get a train there in time. Why on earth did I get involved in all this?'

'Calm yourself, Vivian, you're being ridiculous,' sighed Miss Metford. 'You were sent here for a purpose. And you're damn well going to fulfil that purpose if it's the last thing you do. Leave that paperwork now, I'll take you into town.'

'How?' I asked, half-expecting her to pull out a broomstick.

'In my car, of course.'

'Your car? You can't drive, surely?'

'I stopped driving a long time ago because I decided there were already too many silly old fools on the road causing accidents without me joining them. But just because I don't doesn't mean I can't.'

'Do you think it will be safe?' I asked, thinking how every single time I saw her she shocked me further.

'It strikes me, my dear, you don't have much choice. And a risky witch like you, too? Can't believe you have the audacity to ask such a question.'

With that she stormed off up the path.

I was left torn. Should I risk both our lives by being driven by an eighty-six-year-old battleaxe in a beaten-up old banger? Or did I risk irreversibly losing precious days needed to secure the success of the campaign?

I didn't have long to ponder. After a few minutes, there was an almighty roar at the end of the path. Grabbing my coat and scarf, I ran down to see what was going on.

There stood the most beautiful, immaculate, shiny Bentley I'd ever seen.

'Jump in, girl,' shrieked Miss Metford, flicking her cigarette ash out of the window, 'what are you standing around waiting for?'

The journey into the city was eventful to say the least. It seemed Miss Metford had clean forgotten about the concept of gears, so we groaned most of the way there in first or second. When I kindly pointed this out to her, she snapped at me, then realising I was right, said, 'Oh yes, I remember, couldn't quite work out why I was going so slowly.'

After that I wished I'd left her growling along in first, as we sped into the city at full speed, with Miss Metford failing to even take her foot off the pedal when we came to traffic lights, which incidentally she thought were for wimps. We drove the wrong way down one-way streets, evidently no entry signs had not been invented the last time Miss M was behind the wheel. For my part, I found it easier to hang on to my seat for dear life while closing my eyes so I couldn't see what was ahead of us. We got there in record time, although it did take a few minutes to convince Mary to come in to the printers with me rather than 'doing a few laps round the block' as she had proposed.

'What marvellous fun, my dear,' she exclaimed as we walked through the doors, me shaking and she straightening her hat. 'Can't believe I've left it so long.'

Fortunately for us the printers were not very busy so, although the man behind the counter grimaced at the thought of printing five hundred leaflets so late on a Friday afternoon, he did concede to getting on with the job at a cost.

'Don't worry about that now, dear,' said Miss M as I nervously handed over the money, 'you'll get it back in time. Right, we've got an hour to kill, where's the nearest pub, laddie?'

The printer pointed out an exclusive-looking wine bar over the road. It was full of fashionable young things sipping cocktails. I was just about to ask about a café, when Mary grabbed my hand, saying it was 'Just the ticket'.

Two cocktails each later, she'd managed to convince everyone in there they simply had to visit the darling little Ivory Meadows and that they really must tell their friends. I was concerned Miss M was too squiffy to drive us home but she rebuked me, saying, 'You do talk some frightful bilge, my dear, it's all for the cause.'

We picked up the leaflets, asking the printer to display one in his window and dropping a few over the road to the newly converted bar staff, then bravely returned to the Bentley. I think the cocktails had given us both a little Dutch courage. I tried to tell Mary we really were in no rush this time, but she told me that was an idiotic thing to say to a woman of eighty-six who had infinitely too much to cram into too little time. She told me she'd keep the leaflets in the boot of her car, promising me the mayor wouldn't dare darken *her* doors, but then screeched the car to a halt.

'Why on earth do you want to take them back to Ivory Meadows in the first place?' she turned to me and asked. 'Everyone in Ivory Meadows knows about Ivory Meadows.'

'Bill and Dennis want to deliver them to passengers on

the train,' I said. 'They plan to return to the city and hand them out on street corners; they've already worked out what they're going to say to people.'

'Those pair couldn't organise a drunken party in a pub. I always say if you want a job doing properly you should do it yourself.'

With this the handbrake went on and we rotated full circle in the traffic, driving in the opposite direction to home. Horns beeped all around but we were gone in a big cloud of smoke before anyone could stop us.

That afternoon and into the night, we visited every pub we could find, posted leaflets through every shop letterbox we stumbled upon, and handed them out to every person who deigned to pass us by.

'What are you doing about the press?' asked Miss Metford, finally.

'I was working on a press release when you arrived. Barbara said she would pass it onto a reporter friend she knows at the start of next week.'

'Next week? I could be dead by next week. We'll do it now ourselves. What time is it?'

I looked at my watch. It was approaching seven o'clock.

'They're a lazy bunch, the press, so there won't be anyone in the offices now. But, having said that, they do like a drink. Let's find their offices and visit the pub nearest to it.'

'I'm not sure we'll be able to persuade them,' I said, hesitantly, as we drove around and eventually pulled up outside The Lark pub.

'Don't you believe it, they'll be duck soup when I've finished with them!'

For once, her crazy logic worked. She walked in with great triumph, sought a table of reporters then ordered me to the bar to get everyone a drink. By the time I returned, slightly flummoxed and completely penniless, she had everyone in hysterics and promising they would not only grace their pages with our news but that they would visit themselves to do a live report. I later learnt she'd threatened to strip to her brassiere if they didn't. I must say the mind boggled.

By the time I managed to drag Mary out of the pub, she could barely stand. She insisted I took the wheel. I hadn't driven in years but the Bentley seemed to purr gently, appreciative of my more gentle touch, and we were back in Ivory Meadows in no time. I collected Rosie, apologising to Barbara for being so late and promising to fill her in on all the details soon. Back at Cherrystone Cottage, Miss Metford seemed to sober up and, promising to take it steady up the lane, she got back behind the wheel. Then she proceeded to roar away at full steam to Metford Manor.

I carried my beautiful, sleepy girl to bed, kissed her goodnight, then flopped into the armchair, exhausted. I had to admire Mary's spirit, even if she did leave me bewildered most of the time. Thanks to her, the campaign had already begun, and if the small section of people we'd spoken to were anything to go by, it looked as though it might just work.

Chapter Eleven

Sure enough, on Monday, our story was in all the local papers. The mayor was furious, everyone else was elated. They were simply amazed that so much had happened. I realised it wasn't important who did what, the only importance was that they felt it was their campaign and, having been so involved at the start, it was like it was their new-born baby.

On the Tuesday everyone was excitedly waiting for an influx of people.

It was deathly quiet, like a ghost town. I wondered if I'd made a grave mistake. I tried to reassure everyone to keep the faith but I had to admit I was a little nervous. What if everything everyone had done had been completely in vain?

Wednesday was a totally different story. Slowly but surely strangers started to drift into the town. A woman brought her grandson who was mad on trains, a courting couple came for the romance of the river, a young man brought his mother who had apparently been here many years before and fallen in love.

That night, every shopkeeper stayed late working tirelessly to dress the town with Christmas decorations. By morning, it was as if every shop window had been sprinkled with fairy dust, filled as they were with tinsel, ornaments, and candles. It seemed like a winter wonderland.

Mick hastily put together his festive cookery classes

after being inundated with enquiries, and George put a sandwich board next to his barge with details of his Santa Specials. Jeremy gathered the choir together for a quick rehearsal ready for their grand carol concert on Sunday evening. He also put a quick call into his friend at the travelling circus. Fortunately they hadn't been re-booked after he'd cancelled it earlier in the month and were delighted to be coming to perform in Ivory Meadows once more. They were so pleased for us they even said they'd bring an old-fashioned carousel and Ferris wheel for free. Everything that had been put on hold was quickly resurrected with added vigour and excitement.

It had been Barbara's idea for Bill to take on the mantle of Father Christmas, arriving on a float made to look like a chimney and being the one to turn on the fairy lights in the town. He begrudgingly agreed, but everyone could see he was secretly delighted to have such a starring role in the festivities. He certainly had the belly for it!

Earlier that day, he'd mustered all his strength to help the vicar bring in an enormous Christmas tree, which now stood proudly at the front of the church, so that it was the first thing people saw as they walked or drove into town.

Rosie was coming home more elated every day from school as it seemed all lessons had been put on hold for the children and teachers to work on their plans for the carnival.

By Friday, people were coming in by the busload. Ian of The Mason Arms had run out of draught beer, Nancy from the café sold out of sausages, and at the greengrocers we were swamped with orders to be picked up the following week.

Gillian had spent all week helping everyone work on their floats for the carnival. I thought she must be exhausted but, quite the opposite; it seemed her creative mind was going into overdrive. She suggested a masked ball would make a grand finale, not only to a wonderful carnival but also to a fabulous week and long slog of the campaign. It would also whet everyone's appetite for the rest of the festivities the whole town had planned right through to Christmas Eve. But she was quite adamant there were to be no witch costumes as, she said, that would be inappropriate under the circumstances. She said she'd already checked the town hall was free and asked if the band could continue to play there after the carnival was over.

Everyone thought she was joking at first but I was thrilled at the idea and suggested we should wear ball gowns and dinner jackets. Soon everyone was nodding in agreement. Bill wasn't sure about the 'monkey suits' as he put it, but he did come round when Barbara told Dennis he'd be wearing one, too. I was rather looking forward to seeing Bill all dressed up. He had been so constant, so kind to me from the moment I arrived.

My delight at wearing a 'princess dress' soon turned to panic when I realised I had neither the time nor the money to go into the city to buy one. I resigned myself to having to wear my trusty black dress, pink shawl, and high heels. I knew people were used to seeing me in that outfit but nonetheless I always did look more dressed up than anyone else. Perhaps my favourite outfit would at last fit in and perhaps at last that would mean that I would fit in, too. The pressure had eased immensely since the witch-hunt had been called off, especially after my public apology from the vicar. A good many people had apologised for distancing themselves from me. Maureen went on and on about how ashamed she was of her appalling behaviour. I just smiled sweetly and told them no offence had been taken.

But then did I really want to just fit in, to just be plain old Vivian Myrtle? I admired people like Miss Metford, people who turned their back on convention and did exactly as they chose. That was a pipe dream. In reality I was just plain old Vivian, who lived in a tumble-down cottage with a cute little girl and baked cherry-flavoured fairy cakes. And really that suited me just fine. My days of being the dark horse were long behind me, it had just taken me a long time to realise that. I was ready for a new start and who knew? Maybe even love. I'd met a lot of good, honest people in Ivory Meadows. They'd restored my faith in human nature, a faith that in all things, good would triumph over evil. Yes, I'd been abused once but everything you do comes back to you threefold. My mother had always told me that. Perhaps my ex-husband was getting his comeuppance now and it was my turn to be set free.

As I sat up in bed, thoughts of tomorrow's carnival and ball flashed through my head like a looped film reel. I found myself gently stroking the patchwork quilt. I'd loved its patterns and textures ever since that very first night I lay under it, wondering what mine and Rosie's future held. I loved the fact it was old and worn. It said a lot about the history of the house. There was a piece of lace that I imagined was once part of an old, beautiful wedding dress; a floral green patch that could have been maternity wear; a bright blue satin piece that had probably been worn to a party; a white broderie-anglaise circle that must have been a christening gown. As I stroked the wools, cottons, and silks I felt the warmth and happiness of all these precious moments when parts of this quilt had been worn and enjoyed.

Before I knew it I had scissors in my hand and was cutting it. I cut panels for a tight, strapless bodice and a full skirt to go underneath. As I watched the fragments of history, like pages of a book, fall to the ground I didn't feel shame or remorse. I felt that all those joyous outfits were crying out to be worn again. Through my cutting of the quilt, they were reborn. I would wear a wedding gown, a party dress, a maternity smock, a graduation cape, a going-away outfit, a christening shawl, a favourite coat, a comfort jumper, a baby's first birthday dress, all in one fabulous ball gown.

Taking my needle and thread, I stitched and sewed until the small hours, creating shape and fluidity, giving new life to these fabrics that had been laid to rest. As the sun rose I tacked off my last stitch and stood back to look at my masterpiece as it hung in front of my wardrobe. The light caught it gently, highlighting one fragment after another. A glimpse of silver stitching here, a chiffon rose there, a gingham square next to a toile de joie picture, a hand-painted daisy, a broad piece of fancy brocade, a delicate floral emblem. There were blues, greens, pinks, lilacs but most of it was azure, the colour of my little girl's eyes. I had never seen that before when it had been a bedspread lying over me. It shone and radiated vitality, good health, and warm feelings. I didn't have to be plain Jane to show the people of Ivory Meadows just who I was and how I felt about them and their beautiful, beautiful town.

I still felt it lacked something though, and I wasn't sure what. It was magnificent but it didn't quite hang right for a ball gown. The sun came from behind a cloud, lighting up the whole room and turning the azure dress to gold. That was it. I ran over to the window and pulled down the net curtains. They were ripped and brown at the bottom from years of listless hanging. It didn't matter; there was no time for frivolities now. I cut them into two petticoats, making sure none of the tattered net could be seen underneath the gown.

Very, very gently I took it down from its hanger and carefully climbed into the skirt then fastened the bodice. It felt soft and warm; it still smelt of sweet sleep and wondrous dreams. Closing my eyes, I walked over to the mirror, trembling as I imagined how it might look.

127

Nervously opening my eyes, I saw a woman in the mirror I barely recognised. She looked younger, fresher-faced than me and yet she seemed as though she had the wisdom of all the years the dress had experienced. Tears rolled down my cheeks, but at last they were great big salt wells of relief and utter, utter happiness.

Excitedly, I ran down the dark corridor to Rosie's room. She was still fast asleep, but I had to show her. She rubbed the sleep out of her eyes and looked at me as if I was a fairytale character who had just stepped out of her book and into her room. She blinked twice to check she wasn't dreaming then jumped up and threw her arms around me.

'Where did you get that dress, Mummy? I love it.'

'Don't you recognise it, Rosie?'

She looked puzzled, it was clearly familiar to her but, understandably, she couldn't quite place where she had seen it, for which I was glad as I didn't want people thinking I'd wrapped an old quilt round me to go out. When I told her she looked stunned.

'That old thing? How did you make it so beautiful?'

In all honesty, I couldn't say what had driven me to make it.

'You realise there's one thing you've forgotten,' said Rosie.

'What?' I asked, thinking I'd left a whole panel out of the back and was exposing myself.

'Your mask.'

Of course, she was right, I had completely forgotten. I sat on the bottom of her bed, disillusioned.

'Don't worry, Mummy, I knew you'd forget. That's why I took matters into my own hands, and made this for you.'

At this, she whisked a dazzling cat mask out of her wardrobe. It looked decidedly like Whisper, only the eye holes were surrounded by pale pink glitter and there were elaborate swirling patterns painted onto the cheeks and huge soft whiskers coming from either side of a pretty pink nose. It was cut away under the nose, to allow me to talk and drink. I knew I had the perfect pastel pink lipstick to finish off my feline fabulousness.

'It's amazing, Rosie. How did you do it?'

'You were so busy running around yesterday, doing everything for everyone else, I knew you wouldn't remember your mask and that you wouldn't really notice if I spent a bit more time in my bedroom than usual. Miss M gave me the glitter, cardboard, elastic, and pens.'

Miss M. I knew she had to be involved. I loved my little girl and wondered if others were as thoughtful as she.

'Thank you, thank you, my darling. Come on then,' I said, playfully tapping her on the bottom, 'we've got things to do.'

'But it's still early, Mummy.'

'I know but I'm making pancakes and cherry sauce for breakfast then you and I are heading down into town early for the carnival.'

'Yes, pancakes and the carnival,' shouted Rosie, jumping up and down. She'd been looking forward to it all week.

When we arrived in town, wrapped up in our hats, gloves, and scarves, it was already bustling with people putting up their stalls and making the finishing touches to their floats. It felt like there was magic in the air; it was going to be a great day after all.

The carnival was officially opened by the vicar; the mayor sadly had been unable to make it. During his address Mr Baker revealed news he had received in a letter that morning. The council had refused planning permission for new development in Ivory Meadows on the grounds that it was an area of historical significance.

We were stunned: we had actually done it. We had

saved our beloved town. Everyone cheered and hugged each other. Barbara and Gillian came running over to me, tears running down their faces.

'We did it, Vivian, we did it!'

We all danced around the streets, clapping and cheering. Men punched their fists in the air in delight. Visitors, who had read about little Ivory Meadows in the newspapers and travelled from far and wide to come to the carnival were coming up and shaking our hands.

It was a spectacular moment.

The vicar gradually quietened everyone down again.

'Not only that, everyone,' he added, with a smile, 'the council has decided to issue a grant for further tourism developments in the town, too, so that the beauty of the original Ivory Meadows can be restored and enhanced for all to enjoy.'

There were further whoops and screams. The whole place seemed to come alive with jubilation. Mrs Donaldson hobbled over to me, her husband in tow.

'I knew I was right about you at the very start, Ms Mrytle,' she said. 'You're a good girl.'

'Come here,' laughed Maureen Sprockett, clutching me to her chest, 'As I said before, I'm sorry I got swept up in all the stories. We're so thrilled with everything you've done.'

'I think we all make a pretty good team.' I smiled, grateful for their kindness and acceptance once again.

The news couldn't have come at a better time.

This meant we could host the train rides, the markets, the nature trails, ghosts hunts, riverboat cruises that we'd dreamed of all those months before. At last visitors would come, not to see the accused butcher working in his shop, or the charred remains of the timber house, but to enjoy the town for what it really stood for.

We had done it, we really had.

130

That afternoon, Ivory Meadows became busier and busier. There were throngs of people, many with different accents, proving our message had been spread far and wide. The whole place seemed to buzz with excitement. Elderly people reminisced as they tucked into minced pies, tourists chatted to locals about what was going on in the town. Children danced and twirled, led of course by my own beloved Rosie, to the old-fashioned fairground organ that Jeremy had convinced one of his circus friends to bring along. Each of the shopkeepers put up a market stall outside their shop, offering Christmas gifts, food, wrapping paper, and handmade cards. The air was filled with the smell of roasted chestnuts and tiny silver bells sang a playful tintinnabulation in the breeze. Mistletoe hung from the trees and red, green and gold bunting zigzagged across the streets. Gillian had a wonderful eye for detail when it came to making the town sparkle. She had come up with most of the ideas for the carnival floats too, and had spent yesterday afternoon visiting each and every one to add her finishing touches.

At 3 p.m., a cheer rose as a spectacular brass band came marching over the bridge into the town, marking the start of the carnival procession. Then the first truck was spotted, with two schoolchildren dressed as Mary and Joseph and a 'baby' in a manger at their knees. Loud 'aaahs' could be heard from the crowd as they passed. They were followed by a truck bearing hobby horses dressed as reindeer, and another full of white-clad snowmen, dressed in top hats and dancing animatedly to a ghetto blaster blaring out Christmas tunes. There was a winter scene, with robins and squirrels made out of papier-mâché, which the children and their teachers had laboured over for hours at school.

A fairy float followed, with Rosie and her schoolfriends waving wildly from the top. More music filled the air and there was even a bleating of sheep to be heard as Mr Taverner, the local farmer, brought some of his livestock on the back of his favourite truck. It had been so very kind of him to let us use his vehicles, and his barns to hide away our floats.

Last, but definitely not least, came Father Christmas, stood at the top of an exquisite chimney, made out of cardboard. That had been Gillian's pride and joy. She'd spent days painstakingly painting on bricks and wrapping ivy around it to make it look realistic. The more people cheered and whooped, the more Father Christmas waved and bellowed 'ho, ho, ho'. I just hoped he didn't overdo it and cause the chimney to topple over! I could see Rosie standing on her float, loving every moment. She clearly had no idea who the smiling, rosy-cheeked man was behind the costume.

As his float reached the church, the music softened and the cheering lulled in anticipation. Then Barbara piped up: 'Ten, nine, eight …'

Everyone counted down until we got to one when, magically, all the fairy lights of the town came on, from the huge star on top of the Christmas tree to the lights strung from one lamppost to another. There was a slight delay in getting the lights to switch on across the bridge but no one minded; everyone was happy to repeat the countdown once again. Then there were gasps of delight as the lights' reflection danced in the river below.

A competition to crown Ivory Meadows' beauty queen was won by a bashful Janice, the library assistant, who managed to trip up as she went to collect her garland.

Apart from those very minor hiccups, the day ran smoothly. Everywhere I looked people were smiling, tucking into toffee apples, riding the carousel and Ferris wheel, laughing at the clowns and stilt walkers.

We all joined together to sing carols around the tree, each clasping a mug of mulled wine. There was a winter garland for every visitor, provided by Gillian, and many people were enjoying Mr Shaw's historical tours of the town, which he made slowly yet steadily on his stick, pausing to reflect on the remains of his own scorched house but happily revealing his pride in his new abode. Later, children played hopscotch while their parents huddled together round my stall, chatting as they soaked up my warming cherry gin and fairy cakes. I had ginger biscuits, hedgerow wine made with wild blackberries, walnut cake, flapjacks, pound cakes and scones, all the local delicacies Miss Metford had told me about, bar of course the infamous pigeon pie and stewed eels. I kept a look out for Mary but she didn't show. I thought, just maybe, she might have ventured into town for a celebration like this. I knew she would be proud of the result.

The carnival closed with an impressive acrobatic display by members of the travelling circus, and a grand finale by the brass band. I packed up my stall and Rosie and I sang all the way back up the hill to our home. We were delighted by the carnival, and the fact the town was really ours again. I had been so desperate to save it, to make something right in our lives at last.

Chapter Twelve

Rosie and I tumbled into our little cottage, both caked in icing sugar and me slightly merry on mulled wine. We snuggled up on the sofa in the kitchen with cups of hot tea and countless stories of the day. We talked animatedly about all that we'd seen, heard, smelt, and tasted, both of us high on adrenaline from our incredible adventure. After half-an-hour, I dragged myself away, telling her I really must change for the ball and that she ought to wash her face before Miss Metford arrived for babysitting duties.

I rushed upstairs to take another look at my dress. It was more stunning than I'd remembered it, hanging there shimmering and delicate, like a true princess gown.

I took a long bath, painted my nails, and pinned back my hair, trying to tame my unruly dark locks, which I normally wore loose. They had grown in the time I'd been here, and I hadn't had chance to visit a hairdresser. I put on far more make-up than usual, I think because I knew no one would see it beneath my mask. It gave me confidence. I hadn't slept last night but didn't feel tired at all.

Gently I took the dress off its hanger and carefully climbed through the nets, wools, silks, cottons, and lace of the skirt before gingerly buttoning up the bodice. I had made it strapless. Normally I never exposed my shoulders but then this wasn't really me tonight.

I looked in the mirror, wondering if I'd overdone it. But the dress smiled back at me. 'If I've made so many other people happy,' she whispered, 'how could I make you sad?'

Slipping on my pink heels, I tottered down to Rosie's room to pick up my mask. The gown made me feel like a lady. I stood in the doorway and said, 'What do you think, Rosie?'

'Mummy,' she exclaimed, stunned, 'you look like the prettiest thing I've ever seen.'

I felt myself blush as I stroked her hair and put her to bed, telling her I wouldn't be home late.

'*Fais de beaux rêves*,' I said, kissing her gently on her cheek.

'Have fun, Mummy,' she sighed, sleepily.

When I got downstairs Miss Metford was at the door, waiting to be let in.

'Little one asleep?' she whispered, and I nodded.

'Good, I can get on with reading my book. I take it everything went well today?'

'More marvellous than I could have possibly imagined,' I cooed as I swanned out the door, turning to wave as Mary rolled her eyes.

Putting on my mask, I made my way down the hill. Tonight I would be someone else from the moment I stepped foot out of the door. I would be Cleopatra, Desdemona, Juliet, Lady Chatterley, Holly Golightly all rolled into one. By the time I reached the town it was getting late. There was an eerie smell of fire and sulphur in the air. The fairy lights had been moved from the bridge to the gates of the town hall. They danced in the dark sky, like entertainers in a ballyhoo, twinkling: 'come in, come in'.

A large banner had been put up outside. It read: 'Ivory Meadows Masked Ball. Come As You Are If You Please, But As Somebody Else Is Better!' Next to it were huge torches burning bright, throwing fighting punches into the moonlit sky.

I blushed at the thought I might be the only feline in a gown. Then I glanced inside. Everywhere I looked there were strange creatures. Birds with great beaks, lions, tigers, wolves, foxes, a pelican, another cat, butterflies, eagles, owls, and even a unicorn. Some were strange souls of the underworld, creatures I had never seen before with eyes and ears in the wrong places, covered in glitter and feathers. There was even an elephant and an enormous, menacing bear. There was an exotic peacock with feathers all around her head and a pink flamingo, balancing on one leg.

The dancing had already begun; the tired wooden floorboards of the old town hall transformed into a glamorous dance floor. Elaborate gowns swirled round and round like crinoline ladies on a mechanical jewellery box. The blur of colour, movement, and music was breathtaking.

Most of the masks were outrageous handmade creations, made from cereal boxes, paint, and string. But by the flicker of the candlelight, they looked eerie and surreal. There were feathers, sequins, tiaras, wands, and long, satin gloves.

I had only been there five minutes when I was approached by an eagle. He looked sinister and all-powerful as he took my shawl and whisked it away to the cloakroom without a word. There was something wildly attractive about this silent, masked man. As he returned I tried to get a better look at those piercing eagle eyes while hiding behind my own cat's eyelashes and whiskers. I recognised them but couldn't place them. They were hazel with sharp black lines around the iris, which made them look big and bold. I blinked bashfully as we danced round the dance floor, my dress making wonderful swishing noises and movements and turning from pink to azure to gold in the soft flickering light. Everyone around us seemed to stop and stare. Suddenly I didn't want to speak, didn't want to look him in the eye for fear he'd mistaken me for another pussycat and this wonderful moment was about to come to an abrupt end. I so wanted to be the lucky kitten.

After several dances, we moved off the dance floor and the animals around us parted to allow us to walk through. He sat me down at a table for two in the corner while he went to the bar for drinks: beer for him, cherry brandy for me. Maybe I was the chosen feline after all. Eventually I felt I had to speak. The anticipation was full of electricity, I thought I could explode into hundreds of gold and azure sparks at any time.

'You know if a black cat crosses your path, it's supposed to bring you luck,' I whispered.

'I must be the lucky one then,' he said.

His voice gave him away; I knew it was Bill. He smiled sheepishly. All his might and intrigue seemed to dissolve in a second. The dark stranger was someone I saw every day. I was no longer the hunted woman, I felt spurned. And yet there was still something about him. His thick-set, eagle eyes, his scent. The smell of his aftershave was evocative, reminding me of love and good times.

'Vivian,' he said. My cover was blown; clearly Rosie's disguise had been easier to see through than I'd thought.

'The thing is, Vivian,' he said, awkwardly clasping his hands on his lap, 'the thing is there's something I've been wanting to tell you for a long time.'

Suddenly it didn't matter that it was trusty old Bill, reliable, kind-hearted, hot-headed Bill, Bill whose great big hands always reeked of raw meat and who didn't care who he offended. Bill, who I loved dearly but had never thought of as attractive, Bill, who was not my type. No, the creature sat before me was a completely different bird. And my feline instinct, in fact every fibre of my body, told me to catch him and gobble him up right now before the candles were blown out and the ball gowns packed away.

'Er, excuse me, Bill,' a sparrow tapped him on the shoulder, 'you got a second, mate? We need a hand getting another cask up to the bar.'

The eagle eyes looked hurt. The moment was gone. He apologised and followed the sparrow out of the town hall.

I sat all alone. For the very first time since arriving at Ivory Meadows, I felt completely lonely. I knew people wondered how I coped in a remote rundown cottage without a husband but I'd always had Rosie and my beautiful house and I had felt no need for anything or anyone else. Suddenly that was no longer enough. I wanted more. And I didn't want to be alone at a ball of dancing, whirling dervishes with fake sequinned faces. I got up to leave, making my way over to the cloakroom to retrieve my shawl.

Suddenly, I was cornered by a wolf. He came up behind me and, without touching me, forced me away from the throngs of bejewelled and gowned people.

'Hello, Cathy,' he said.

Cathy? It felt as if I hadn't been called that in years.

'You look amazing, the belle of the ball. You have no idea how pleased I am to see you at long last.'

My dress felt tight. All its different fabrics became hot and uncomfortable, each fighting to be the most important, the most prominent. I could hardly hear him over the sound of my raging dress. I couldn't breathe. I knew I had to get out so I fled deep into the darkness, back up the hill to the safety of my home and daughter like a hunted woman. I no longer wanted to be the belle of the ball. I wanted to be invisible.

Fortunately the masked man didn't follow.

Chapter Thirteen

I dashed into Cherrystone Cottage and flung the door shut behind me, pushing my body against it to try to block out the gravity of what had just happened.

It was as if my whole world had rocked then stood still.

Miss Metford slowly raised her eyes from her book, carefully took out her bookmark and placed it inside. 'What on earth is the matter, dear girl, you look like you've seen a ghost.'

'He was there,' I mumbled, 'there at the ball. What am I to do? Rosie, Rosie, is she OK?'

'Rosie, yes, haven't heard a murmur since the moment you left.'

I raced up to her room, crashing through the door, expecting the bed to be empty, my golden girl to be gone.

Of course, she was lay there, sound asleep, gently sighing in her tranquil slumber. I sat with her for a moment, softly stroking her hair. I had to protect her, she had no idea what we were about to be up against. Frantically, I began to grab a few of her clothes, her favourite toy and book, stuffing them into a bag. It was time for us to move on again, the game was over, we'd been caught; we had to leave. I was devastated. I loved it here; I loved it with every sinew of my body. This was my town now; I deserved the right to live here peacefully with my clever, brave daughter. But it seemed fate had determined that was not to be the case. I suppose I was naïve, simply changing my name, we were bound to be found sooner or later.

Why is life so very cruel? In saving Ivory Meadows, I'd endangered everything I'd created for myself and my child. If I'd have just stayed quiet, maybe we could have carried on as we were, although then perhaps there would have been no town to carry on in.

Mary was behind me in a flash. It always took me by surprise how sprightly she was for her age. 'What on earth are you doing, Vivian?'

'I'm packing, Mary.'

'I can see that, even though I'm still wearing these silly reading glasses. My question is why? Who did you say was back? Was it old Johnson? He's a nasty piece of work but don't worry yourself, Vivian.'

'No, it wasn't Mr Johnson,' I said, moving up into my room, where I grabbed my jewellery and a few photographs of Rosie and threw them into the bag. 'It was someone entirely more dangerous.'

'Oh,' said Mary, her face dropping, 'you mean your husband?'

'My ex-husband,' I rebuked her, 'and yes, he'll be here within minutes so I suggest you get yourself home and safe before Rosie and I take off.'

'You can't just slip away into the night like a pair of shadows.'

'Why ever not? We've done it before, we'll do it again. My job as a mother is to keep Rosemary safe and I've failed miserably. Sounding off my big mouth to save this town has put my precious little girl at risk. I've been a fool, but it won't happen again. You've been a good friend and a great help, Mary, but I need you to go now, move out of my way.'

She shrugged her shoulders like a petulant child before opening her mouth to speak.

'Now!' I shouted, waking up Rosemary, who came

running to my room, asking what was wrong.

I whisked her into my arms, taking comfort and courage from the smell of her long golden hair, and carrying her downstairs, bundling on her coat and pushing her into shoes.

She sleepily whispered, 'Not again, Mummy, I thought this was our home, our real, forever home.'

It broke my heart but I had to stay resolute. 'No, Rosie, it's time to go, I've got your things, get moving.'

'But I like it here, I've made friends here, everyone is lovely, and what about my cat?'

'Take Whisper with you, my darling,' sighed Miss Metford, returning from the lounge, carrying the cat and placing him gently in Rosie's arms.

And with that, with no further argument, Mary was gone.

Pulling my coat over my now-ridiculous ball gown, I loaded the bags onto my back and opened the door. The cold air hit me like a tidal wave, forcing me to face the reality of our situation. Where were we going to go? That didn't matter now – we just had to get out before it was too late. Suddenly I remembered I'd left my mother's locket in the bedroom drawer. Telling Rosie not to move, I dashed upstairs to grab it.

Returning moments later, everything had changed.

There he was, stood in my kitchen, holding my little girl in his arms as she nuzzled into his neck. He was no longer a wolf but just – Jack. But he may as well have kept his wolf costume on.

'Put her down,' I screamed at him, clawing at my child, 'let her go, we're leaving, we want nothing to do with you.'

'Cathy, calm down, let's talk this through, it's taken me so long to find you. I've searched every day since the moment you left. We need to sort things out, make them right, for both of us, and for Lily.'

'There's nothing to sort out,' I bellowed, 'it's over, you knew that the day you killed our daughter.'

And, with that, the memories and the enormity of my grief filled every part of my body, every part of the room, so that I could hardly breathe. It all came flooding back like a tidal wave, knocking me off my feet like a heap of old, worn-out fabric in the middle of the floor.

Oh yes, I remembered, I remembered those long seven weeks watching her every move. It was the waiting that was the hardest part. While pregnant, I couldn't wait for her to be born. And my impatience had brought on an early labour. As my waters broke, I screamed, 'It's not time, she's not ready.' My distress, my sheer knowledge that it wasn't our time nearly killed us both.

For days, Jack watched and waited for either of us to come round, with the dreadful fear he could lose us both. Eventually after three days, he said I awoke with a start, jumped up and said, 'Where's Rosemary?'

We hadn't decided on a name, and Jack was amazed I knew it was a girl.

I hobbled over to see my poor, deformed baby, my child who I'd forced into the world before she'd had chance to finish building herself.

And yet she wasn't deformed, she was perfect. Ten tiny fingers, ten tiny toes. I longed to pick her up, hold her in my arms. I truly believed I could heal her, just with a mother's touch. I was the one at fault, the one who'd got her into trouble, surely I was the one who could and should fix her? Each time I ventured near the ventilator I was ushered away by nurses. It was my baby, why were they keeping her from me?

Was I that bad a mother?

Jack did his best to reassure me but, as the weeks passed, it seemed less and less likely she was going to get off that horrid wired-up machine. In time, I carefully put my hand into the incubator and held her fragile fingers, willing her to live. I needed her to make it. Even though I'd never held her, I already knew I couldn't manage without her. I spent every moment of every day and night sat at her side, cradling the glass, begging her to hold on.

Jack said it was time to let Rosie lead her own life in another place. That it was time to turn off the machine.

I ranted and raved. There was no way that could happen, not while I truly believed in my heart of hearts that she was still alive, albeit kept so by machines.

Jack said what I was doing was wrong, that it was unfair both to Rosie and to him, and to me.

The doctors sided with Jack. It seemed everyone was against me, everyone except my beautiful little girl who was clearly willing me not to let her go. The doctors suggested we hold a baptism for our baby girl. Our family came but I sat, motionless, in the corner. I felt like this was their way of saying goodbye and I wanted no part in saying goodbye to a baby who was not ready to leave.

One night we argued until dawn. By morning Jack was lying on the floor, blood on his face. To this day I don't know what happened. But as he picked himself up and wiped himself down, I knew there and then it was over.

I never went to the hospital again. Jack had murdered my baby girl.

We continued to argue constantly. He told me I was a paranoid, neurotic mother and that I should think of what this was doing to Lily, our six-year-old.

I thought long and hard about it and decided exactly what I needed to do: leave. That night I picked Lily up from her bed, took the cash from Jack's wallet, and fled into the night. I didn't even take a change of clothes. We jumped on an underground train, taking us to an entirely different district of London. For a while we wandered the streets, searching for an answer. Then we stumbled upon a women's refuge and thankfully they took us in. Speaking to the other women I realised I myself, like so many of them, had been a battered wife, mentally tortured by my cruel, heartless husband.

After a couple of days one of the women accidentally told me the counsellor at the refuge felt I needed 'clinical help'. Fearing the worst, I picked up Lily, our clean clothes we'd kindly been given and walked out of the door. That night she slept, fitfully, in my arms in the doorway of a church. I didn't close my eyes for a second, for fear of what would become of us.

The next morning I took her to a coffee shop so she could have a glass of juice and I could have a cup of tea and think about our future. As I sat there gazing into my cup, it seemed bottomless. There seemed nowhere for us to go apart from back to Jack.

Resigned to that being our only option, I opened the newspaper and flicked aimlessly through the pages. I came across an advert that had been circled in red pen. It was for a pretty little white cottage for rent in a tiny town called Ivory Meadows. It was called Cherrystone Cottage. I instantly knew it had to be mine. I called from a telephone box outside the café and two hours later Lily and I were on the train on our way to our new home.

When I spoke to the woman at the other end of the phone, I told her my name was Vivian Myrtle and that I had a daughter called Rosemary.

I have no idea where such a strange name came from but it stuck and it seems much more my own now than Catherine Mills ever did. Why I gave my poor elder daughter the name of my tiny deceased baby, I'll never know. But she never complained, she never questioned what I was doing, just went along cheerfully for an adventure with Mummy where we each took on the name of fairy princesses. She very rarely mentioned her little sister, only when we found the tiny skull in the garden and again when she was delirious with fever. I never brought her up in conversation, although I realise now I probably should have done. It was a subject I found far too difficult to talk about, especially on a level that a seven-year-old could understand. Lily did, however, often wonder about her father, thoughts I'd try to lightly bat away as if we were on some jolly holiday.

'Cathy, talk to me,' said Jack, shaking me out of my reverie. 'You can't just keep running away. I need you, I miss you.

'I've looked everywhere for you. I even thought I'd traced you to Ivory Meadows a couple of months ago but the vicar convinced me there was no one here that matched your description. You don't know, you don't know what it has been like, not knowing where you were, whether you were alive, even?'

'I've been so worried about you.' He sighed, his voice breaking softly. 'How are you, Cathy? How's Rosie?'

I cast him a look.

'Don't worry. Your friend Miss Metford has kindly told me all about how you two have been getting along. I understand a lot more than I used to now.'

'But …'

I tried to speak yet the words wouldn't come. Aftershave. It was the same as earlier, I knew I'd recognised it on Bill. How strange they should both choose the same scent. It smelt good, reminding me of happier times when I'd loved and been loved in return.

'But …'

I felt if I didn't say it my whole body would explode.

Jack looked caringly into my eyes, willing me to speak. I could see he wasn't an abuser, a torturer, a liar or a murderer. How had he become such a villain in my mind? How had those seeds of doubt placed by the women in the hostel, the real victims, grown so far out of proportion? He had only ever wanted the best for me. All those years I'd loved and cared for him came flooding

147

back. How he'd wooed me with flowers, wine, and trips to Paris. Not that I'd needed much persuasion. As soon as he'd held the door open for me that very first day, our eyes had met and his hand brushed my shoulder and that was it. I was hooked. He was hooked.

Even when our poor baby girl lay helpless in her incubator in hospital, Jack was only trying to get me to leave her bedside occasionally, just to eat and to sleep. I'd seen it as a slap round the face when he'd accused me of suffering from post-natal depression. I'd become angry, animated, roaring at him like a wild animal about the fact he had no idea how I felt. Actually, now I could see, he had been right all along. It hadn't been an accusation at all, merely a suggestion, borne out of kindness, not hostility. And it must have taken courage to say those words, words that had been for my benefit, our benefit. Everything had been for us, as a family. Why had I not seen that before?

'But ...' I tried again, 'but Rosie had to go. It wasn't her time. In switching off her life-support machine, you weren't evil or cruel, you were just doing what was right for you, me and Lily. And for Rosie, too.'

With that my whole body deflated. It felt as if I was left swimming in an enormous flood of tears that seemed to run across the kitchen tiles and through the door, creating a pool in the garden.

It was pure and utter relief. I had been hiding for too long, pretending there was a sort of magic in our cottage that was protecting us, building up a defensive barrier against the cruel truth of our past. I could see now I'd developed a whimsical way of seeing things to shelter Lily, and indeed myself, from our harsh reality. The guilt and grief I had felt was so huge, it left me void of anything but despair. I should have been the adult, the parent, sharing my role with Jack equally in the decision to switch off Rosie's life support machine. Instead I'd shied away from the reality of our situation, throwing out my own

148

accusations like daggers across the room and ranting like a child deprived of its toy. I was filled with a kind of madness, I can see it now, when I look back.

In the days preceeding Rosemary's death, my mind had gone blank, my feelings numbed as I stumbled blindly through each waking hour and fretful night. Every time I tried to think straight, to lift myself up out of the dense fog in my head, I became more confused, more empty and defunct.

And yet, as soon as we were on our way to Ivory Meadows, I had felt a new lease of life. The moment I uttered my false name, I realised that, by playing this fairy-tale character, I didn't have to play myself. I could be someone entirely different: a kind, caring woman who stood up for what she believed in and protected it, no matter what. My mother had always been full of fanciful ideas, with her bizarre notions and potions. I'd found I'd been thinking of her, and her strange ways, more in the last few months than I had since she'd died three years ago. I guess that questioning your role as a mother makes you think back to your own upbringing. Perhaps it was the madness of the previous months, or what I now recognise was probably depression, but the imaginary story I'd fabricated seemed to make perfect sense to me. Now I saw it was a kind of craziness, the vicar had seen it, as had Barbara and Mary, although they each dealt with it in their own ways.

At last, this make-believe world I'd created was crumbling around me, and I couldn't have cared less. I no longer needed it. I had changed, everything had changed.

It had taken such a long time to even begin to come to terms with the loss of my baby girl, far longer than I'd been able to carry her in my belly. It was a loss I should have shared with my husband, a loss that should have brought us closer together in our struggle against it all. Instead, in my desperate guilt, I had tried to shift my blame

149

onto someone else. And naturally, that culpability was passed to the one I loved the most.

Jack picked me up and held me tight in his arms. He felt so strong, so capable, as if nothing in the world would go wrong when he was there. Why hadn't I felt like this before?

'I'm so sorry,' I whispered, my words muffled as I burrowed my head into his neck the way I used to. 'I'm so very, very sorry.'

'You did what you had to do to cope. I just wish I could have done more to help you.'

'You did so much,' I sobbed, 'if it hadn't been for you, I'd still be by Rosie's incubator, two empty corpses side by side.

'I realise now I was running away from myself, not you. I felt so compelled to try to save this little town, having failed so miserably to save my own little baby. And strangely, in doing so, I've built a life for myself and Lily here. Lily and I have actually managed to find happiness again.

'But there's not a day gone by when I haven't thought about you, and missed you. Even though, in my head, you were the villain and I hated what you'd done, I still couldn't stop loving you. And that made me hate myself and you even more. Can you understand any of that?'

'Yes, Cathy, I can. I've gone over and over that night I got you to sign the consent form to turn off the life support machine. I have been racked with guilt, wondering if I put too much pressure on you to do the right thing. But you have to remember I have been grieving since the moment our baby girl came into our lives too soon, too. The sun will never shine quite so brightly for me without Rosie.

'But for me the grief has been threefold. Because in doing what the doctors advised, in doing what I felt was best, what I always believed you knew in your heart of hearts was best, I lost two daughters and a wife.'

150

'Oh, Jack,' I wept, 'how can you ever forgive me?'

'In the way I hope you'll forgive me?'

'Mummy, Daddy,' yelled Lily, 'does this mean we're a family again?'

'It certainly does,' said both Jack and I, at almost the same time.

We smiled at each other, realising that old flame was still there after all these years.

'And do I still get to keep the cat?'

We laughed.

The next morning I awoke early and the house seemed still and quiet. Normally Rosie, sorry Lily, would be pestering me for breakfast. Had it all been just a dream?

No. Jack was still there at my side, holding my hand, his head sweetly nuzzled into my neck the way he always slept. We had talked for hours after Lily had gone to bed, tentatively at first, each exploring how the other had changed, then rejoicing in what still remained; how our love had grown stronger over the passing of time and the poignancy of grief. Jack marvelled at all that Lily and I had achieved, and I cried when I learnt how his life had been put on hold while he'd spent every waking moment searching for us.

Now that he lay here by my side, it felt as if we'd never been apart. I tenderly loosened my hand from his, pulled the cover over him then tiptoed out of the bedroom door.

When I got to Lily's door I hesitated. What impact would all this have had on my lovely, caring little girl?

Gently I opened the door and it creaked softly the way it always did. There on the bed lay Lily, just as before, only somehow different. She looked older, wiser, and more peaceful than ever. Hearing the door creak, she blinked, sat up and rubbed her eyes.

'Do you love me, Mummy?' she asked.

'Oh yes,' I answered, rubbing her cheeks, which were, once again, covered in glitter.

'As much as Rosie?'

'My Lily, I love you for you, just the way you are. I've never wanted you to be anything other than you. You've always been my Lily, my world, my everything. You are a very brave young lady, and you always make me hugely proud.'

She shrugged and tried to smile.

'Oh, my darling, I'm so very sorry. I should never have given you that name when we got here. I never explained to you fully what was going on, but you went along with it, you were such an angel. Rosie couldn't stay with us so we'll never know whether she was going to grow up to be such a beautiful, smart girl as you. But remember a little bit of your sister lives on in you, just as she does in me and Daddy. It's OK to talk about her, it's OK to talk about anything now. We're not hiding or running any more. We can be ourselves again, my lovely Lily.'

'Oh, Mummy,' she said, sitting up to give me a hug. 'Does that mean we're going to keep seeing Daddy?'

'We are, sweetheart. Have you missed him terribly?'

Lily nodded solemnly and I felt my heart would break. My cheerful, sunshine girl had so carefully hidden away her pain to look after her broken, angst-ridden mother. I felt guilt searing through my veins again. How could I have been so blind as to think my eldest girl was happy without her baby sister, her father, even her own name?

But then I stopped myself. Guilt eats away at you. I know that only too well. And hadn't I built a nice life here for us in Ivory Meadows? We had had a lot of fun and together, we'd been on a journey that had perhaps helped to heal us both. And yet at the same time, I'd felt a yearning, an emptiness in my heart. I tried to fill it by keeping busy, surrounding myself with people and the fight to save the town. Last night, for the first time, I realised what that gap in my life was. It was Jack. The force of my feelings had hit me hard and I'd clung to him in bed like a helpless child, tears streaming down my cheeks as he kissed each one away. We promised to try to keep each other, and Lily, safe and happy from now on. The raw pain and the torment of losing Rosie would still be present, something we woke to every morning and lay in bed thinking of each night, but it would be a sorrow we would share together now, a suffering which could perhaps soften a little with the passing of time. She was our girl. She would, forever, be with us in our thoughts and in our hearts.

Now, I turned again to our beautiful daughter Lily, the sole surviving product of the love and devotion we once again felt for each other.

'Although times have been hard, you've always made it so much easier with your cheeky grin and freckles. And all that hair, like the sun itself had fallen from the sky and landed on top of your head. I just hid you for a while behind Rosie. We can think of Rosie as a beautiful star twinkling over us in the night sky. But now it's time for you to shine and be the amazing girl that you are – as pretty as sunset and as bright as sun-up.'

We hugged and hugged, tears rolling down our cheeks until I said, 'Pancakes for breakfast?'

'With Daddy?'

'You bet!'

We tumbled downstairs together to find Jack already in the kitchen, mixing flour, eggs, and milk.

'When did you learn to cook?' I asked, slipping my hand around his waist.

'When I had to become self-sufficient.' He laughed.

With cherry jam dribbling down our faces, we laughed and cried together all morning, reminiscing about the past, fondly talking about Rosie, catching up where we left off

153

and making plans for our future.

At last, Lily and I were home, with the man we had both been yearning for all this time, in the beautiful and now flourishing town of Ivory Meadows.

The End

Other Accent Press Titles

For more information about **Zoe Chamberlain**
and other **Accent Press** titles
please visit

www.accentpress.co.uk

Printed in Great Britain
by Amazon.co.uk, Ltd.,
Marston Gate.